THE SHOOTING SCRIPT®

HUGO

M000312243

THE SHOOTING SCRIPT®

HUGO

Screenplay by John Logan

Based on the Book Entitled
The Invention of Hugo Cabret by Brian Selznick

Introduction by John Logan

Foreword by Brian Selznick

**newmarket press
for itbooks**
AN IMPRINT OF HARPERCOLLINS PUBLISHERS

A Newmarket Shooting Script® Series Book

Screenplay and production notes © 2011 Paramount Pictures Corp.
Pictures copyright © 2011 GK Films LLC. All rights reserved.
Foreword by Brian Selznick © 2011 by Brian Selznick
Introduction by John Logan © 2011 by John Logan
All rights reserved. Used by permission.
Printed in the United States of America.

No part of this book may be used or reproduced in any manner whatsoever without written permission except in the case of brief quotations embodied in critical articles or reviews. For information address HarperCollins Publishers, 10 East 53rd Street, New York, NY 10022.

Books may be purchased for educational, business, or sales promotional use. For information address HarperCollins publishers, 10 East 53rd Street, New York, NY 10022.

First Edition

Library of Congress Cataloging-in-Publication Data is available upon request.

ISBN 978-0-06-220277-2

12 13 14 15 16 10 9 8 7 6 5 4 3 2 1

The Newmarket Shooting Script® Series is a registered trademark.

CONTENTS

FOREWORD

BY BRIAN SELZNICK

Sometimes, from what I hear, authors are unhappy with the film adaptations of their books. Sometimes authors feel that the alterations made to their original stories obscure their vision and leave them feeling alienated and unhappy. That's what I hear anyway.

As for me, let's just say that when John Logan asked me to write the preface to his beautiful screenplay adaptation of my book, *The Invention of Hugo Cabret*, I jumped at the chance.

My book is about a boy named Hugo who lives secretly in the walls of a train station in Paris in 1931. He meets a bitter old man who turns out to be the legendary filmmaker Georges Méliès. (In real life, Méliès ended up penniless, working in his later years in a toy booth in the Gare Montparnasse in Paris). My book is 530 pages long and includes 300 pages of illustrations.

The Invention of Hugo Cabret was intended to celebrate the history of cinema and to celebrate Méliès, one of its greatest and most overlooked pioneers. But really, for me, it's about the importance of *books*. In fact, the book itself, the object in your hand when you are reading my original story, is actually an important part of the plot. As a result, I thought the book I made was unfilmable. But then Martin Scorsese called! That's when I first thought to myself, "Hmmm, maybe this *can* work on the screen."

I had the great pleasure of reading John Logan's screenplay from the very first draft. Right away, he had come up with a new ending that expanded on and completed one of the central scenes in my story, a conversation between the two main characters, Hugo and Isabelle, about what their purpose in life might be. That's when I knew the screenplay was going to be brilliant. John kept the dialogue spare. I love the fact that there are no spoken words for the first several minutes of the movie. The world of the Parisian train station, Hugo's world, unfolds visually, just like it does in my book.

The picture sequences I drew are almost like black-and-white storyboards that move us through space, zoom in on important objects, and cut from moment to moment to move the action forward. This is all accomplished through the one simple yet amazing technology that books offer: the turning of the page.

Part of John's challenge was to take my picture sequences and turn them into text, which would then be turned back into visuals by Scorsese using the latest technology the cinema has to offer: 3D. John also had to telescope and change details from my book in order to keep the story moving on screen. Thus some characters had to be cut and others added, but always for a reason.

Sometimes, though, I admit that I just couldn't understand the changes. For instance, in my original book, Hugo keeps the fact that he lives in the walls of the train station as a closely guarded secret. After he meets Isabelle, who wants to know where he lives, he goes out of his way to hide the answer from her. Isabelle manages to track Hugo down, wrestle him to the floor, and force him to explain what's going on. It's a rough, uncomfortable scene, and it unfolds over many pages. In the screenplay, however, Isabelle simply says, "Hugo, where do you live?" while the two characters are standing on a bridge. Hugo points toward the train station and says, "There."

What?? I thought. That's it??

I was really disappointed by this scene as written on the page. But I happened to be on the set in London when Scorsese filmed it with Asa Butterfield and Chloë Grace Moretz. The kids were standing on a fake bridge in front of a green screen that would eventually become the River Seine. I watched Asa and Chloe perform this moment together. Chloe gently asked the question, "Hugo...where do you live?" and Asa paused. You could see him making a thousand decisions in his mind, deciding whether or not to trust her.

John had actually provided these directions in the script, which at first I'd overlooked: *"He stops. Looks at her. Should he tell her? Should he trust her? Yes."* Slowly Asa lifted his arm and pointed behind him. "There," he said very quietly. Tears came to my eyes as he pointed towards the train station. It was so simple and yet so moving. And it was perfect for the screen, just as John knew it would be.

As I've said, my book celebrates the movies, but it's really about the importance of books. John Logan, in adapting my book for the screen, performed a kind of magic trick. He took my story and turned it inside out. He turned it into a story that feels like it was always meant to be a *movie*, and yet he also took the time to celebrate books. Hugo and Isabelle are constantly talking about reading and writing; they visit bookstores and libraries; they name drop authors like Jules Verne and Robert Louis Stevenson and characters from literature like Jean Valjean and Robin Hood. The fact that this all happens in the context of a gigantic, glorious, heartfelt, cinematic masterpiece just makes it all the more meaningful.

—December 2011

INTRODUCTION

BY JOHN LOGAN

*H*ugo was a gift to me.

From first to last, I felt I had been given something precious: adapting a book I love; working with inspiring colleagues I admire; getting to tell this wise and benevolent story; just living in this world for a few years.

In *The Invention of Hugo Cabret* Brian Selznick made a beautiful book. His austere and haunting illustrations work in concert with his deceptively simple story of a young French orphan making a home for himself. It's an ingenious work that thrills on many levels: dazzling adventure story; fiendishly-clever mystery; sweeping historical pageant; evocation of a bygone era of moviemaking. But at every turn the face of that lost, sad boy, Hugo Cabret, gazes out at you, imploring, seeking, challenging. It will touch you, this book. I am grateful for its part in my life and for Brian Selznick's constant support and friendship.

When Martin Scorsese and Graham King asked me to adapt Brian's book, I said yes instantly. The chance to work with my *Aviator* comrades again, and on this movie, was irresistible. I thank them for bringing me this five-year challenge. As always with an adaptation, the first job was finding an organizing principle around which to fashion the screenplay. Give the book to five different screenwriters, and you will get five different versions of the story, five different movies. So what was it about the book that touched me? What amused and excited me? What makes it a work of cinema and not a work of literature? In discussing the book with Marty, we kept returning to the face of Hugo; to the story of that damaged boy. We began to circle an idea: a film of damaged characters that are finally healed by their courage, their imagination, and their compassion. At heart Hugo is a boy who fixes things: clocks, machines, and people. And at the conclusion of the story he earns his happy ending because of all the good he has done for the other characters. He is selfless and kind and inspires kindness in others.

Throughout the process, Marty and I spoke about Truffaut's *The 400 Blows* and the films of René Clair. I began to draw parallels from Hugo's story to those of the great Dickensian orphans: Pip; Little Nell; Oliver Twist; Little Dorrit; David Copperfield. Those books became additional touchstones for me: mostly for their unapologetic toughness and their unwillingness to condescend to the young characters. Dickens was never afraid to make the pain real for his literary children. He didn't wink and tell his readers it was all going to be fine in the end; frequently it wasn't. I watched the two great David Lean Dickens film adaptations and a fair amount of Carol Reed as well; getting a sense for the unsentimental sentiment they were able to create on screen. There's nothing weepy about their work, but it makes you weep. That seemed right for *Hugo*.

All through this gradual excavation of the screenplay, Marty was generously introducing me to the world of Georges Méliès and silent film. My synapses jumped to keep up with his, and—as always with Marty—his dizzying joy for cinema and storytelling was infectious and inspiring.

I am inordinately proud of this film. And while I'm hardly impartial, I feel there's something genuinely enchanted about *Hugo*; something unique about why we make movies in the first place; about our need for magic. There's nothing particularly ironic or post-modern about the script. It's meant to be earnest storytelling. This is a script that leads with the heart; there was no other way to do it.

—December 2011

<u>THE INVENTION OF HUGO CABRET</u>

Screenplay

By

John Logan

Based on the book

By

Brian Selznick

VIOLET PAGES
Issued: Dec 1, 2010

SALMON PAGES
Issued: November 22, 2010

BUFF PAGES
Issued: November 8, 2010

GOLDENROD PAGES
Issued: October 18, 2010

GREEN PAGES
Issued: September 9, 2010

YELLOW PAGES
Issued: August 31, 2010

PINK PAGES
Issue: July 5, 2010

BLUE PAGES
Issued: June 18, 2010

SHOOTING SCRIPT
Issued: May 5, 2010

1   INT. TRAIN STATION -- GRAND HALL - DAY   1

From far above it looks like a great clockwork.

We are looking down on the Grand Hall of the Paris Train
Station.

It is crowded.

People bustle back and forth.

Like the gears and wheels of a clock.

A precise, beautiful machine.

We float down...

Under the great iron girders...

Moving through the station...

Past kiosks and shops...

Weaving among commuters...

Heading toward the trains and platforms in the distance...

Finally moving up to...

A huge clock suspended from the ceiling of the station...

Behind the ironwork dial we see a face peering out.

HUGO CABRET looks at us. He is a serious-looking boy of
around 12. Long hair.

It is 1931.

2   INT. TRAIN STATION -- TUNNELS - DAY   2

Hugo turns away from the dial and moves through the tunnels
behind the clock.

A serpentine maze of passageways.

Behind the walls.

Hugo's secret world.

(CONTINUED)

2   CONTINUED: 2

<u>We move with him</u> as he goes quickly up and down spiral
staircases ... ducking through tiny openings ... swerving in
and out of dark passages ... up and down, back and forth...

Like an elaborate game of Chutes and Ladders.

He finally stops. Peers through another clock dial into a
different part of the station.

He sees...

A TOY BOOTH.

Bedraggled and struggling. A counter filled with windup toys,
dolls and little games.

<u>GEORGES</u>, a grim old man with a white goatee, sits at the
counter of the booth.

Hugo watches.

<u>ISABELLE</u> appears from inside the booth and talks to the old
man. She has a book under her arm.

She is a lively, imaginative girl about Hugo's age. She has
a charming Louise Brooks haircut.

Isabelle argues a bit with Georges. He snaps at her. Upset,
she hurries off.

Hugo watches her go.

Then he turns his gaze to the toys on the counter.

He sees the old man aimlessly wind a TOY MOUSE. It skitters
across the counter. The old man crosses his arms. Falls
asleep.

Hugo stares at the toy mouse.

Then he moves.

He skitters through a series of passages and opens an air
vent. He carefully climbs out, into the station...

3   INT. TRAIN STATION -- TOY BOOTH - DAY   3

Hugo creeps to the Toy Booth.

The toy mouse is there on the counter.

Georges still appears to be asleep.

Hugo stops.

Waits.

Looks around.

Carefully reaches for the toy mouse--

But--

Georges' eyes snap open--!

He grabs Hugo--!

Hugo drops the toy mouse--

It falls and breaks--

Hugo struggles. Georges holds him firm.

> GEORGES
> Got you at last. This isn't the first
> time you've stolen from me, is it, my
> little thief?! Quick, empty your
> pockets!

> HUGO
> You're hurting me!

> GEORGES
> Empty your pockets or I'll call the
> Station Inspector! Do as I say!

The threat of the Station Inspector <u>terrifies</u> Hugo.

He quickly empties his pockets. Dozens of objects. Screws.
Nails. Bits of metal and glass. Tiny pieces of clockworks.
Cogs and wheels.

> GEORGES
> And the other one.

> HUGO
> There's nothing in it!

3   CONTINUED: 3

                         GEORGES
                    (Starts to call)
              Where's the Station Inspector...?!

Hugo empties his last pocket. Reluctantly giving up a
precious object:

An old cardboard NOTEBOOK.

Georges flips through it--

He sees words, pictures, engineering diagrams, schematics,
clockwork drawings--

Then he suddenly stops flipping--

Shocked--

It is like he has seen a ghost--

He stares at a page of the notebook--

A drawing of a MECHANICAL MAN man with clockwork innards. An
elegant and complex mechanism.

But it is the <u>face</u> of the mechanical man that transfixes.
Strangely passive and yet expressing a sort of sadness. Or
wisdom.

It is a haunting face.

Georges thumbs through a few pages of the notebook.

It is like an old *FLIPBOOK*.

The mechanical man's face changes perspective as the pages
flip past. Like primitive animation.

Georges stops.

Slowly closes the notebook.

                         GEORGES
                      (whispers)
                  Ghosts...

He turns to Hugo. Sadness turning to rage.

                                                    (CONTINUED)

3   CONTINUED: 3

                         GEORGES
              Did you draw these pictures?!
                   (no response)
              <u>Did</u> <u>you</u> <u>draw</u> <u>these</u> <u>pictures</u>?!

Hugo tries to pull away.

Georges' grip is iron.

                         GEORGES
              Where did you steal this?!

                         HUGO
              I didn't steal it!

                         GEORGES
              A thief <u>and</u> a liar.

Georges releases Hugo.

                         GEORGES
              Get out of my sight.

                         HUGO
              Give me my notebook!

                         GEORGES
              It is no longer <u>your</u> notebook, it
              is <u>my</u> notebook and I'll do with it
              what I want. Maybe I'll just burn
              it.

                         HUGO
              No!

                         GEORGES
              Then tell me who did the drawings.

Hugo glares at him. Says nothing.

Georges suddenly SLAMS his fist down on the counter. All the
toys jump.

                         GEORGES
              GET OUT OF HERE, YOU LITTLE THIEF!

His shout echoes around the station...

Reverberating from walls ... ceiling ... girders ... windows
... all around the cavernous station...

                                                    (CONTINUED)

3   CONTINUED: 3

To the ears of...

MAXIMILIAN -- an enormous Doberman Pinscher.

His ears perk up. His head tilts dangerously. He glares.
Listening. Alert.

THE STATION INSPECTOR, his master, glances down at him.

The Station Inspector is a tall man in a bottle-green coat,
flamboyantly frightening ... Made even more menacing by a
squeaking metal brace that bolts around one leg. He's like a
partly mechanical man.

He and Maximilian are twin figures of implacable severity.

                    STATION INSPECTOR
              Maximilian? ... What do you hear?
              ... Do you hear ... malfeasance?!

The dog growls dangerously.

Strains at his leash.

The Station Inspector smiles.

                    STATION INSPECTOR
          GO!

He releases the terrible hound--

Maximilian bolts--

The Station Inspector follows -- he is remarkably agile with
his iron-shrouded leg, moving like an elegant spider--

Maximilian tears through the station--

People leap aside in shock and terror as the ferocious dog
sweeps past--

The Station Inspector spiders after him, his boots pounding
over the polished floors, his leg brace squeaking wildly--

Maximilian's nails slips as he rounds a corner, he almost
spins out, but doesn't--

For ahead he sees--

Hugo.

                                                    (CONTINUED)

3   CONTINUED: 3

At the toy booth.

Hugo sees the dog and sprints--

Running away in desperation--

Maximilian pursues--

4   INT. TRAIN STATION -- GRAND HALL - DAY   4

The chase is on!

Huge weaves through pedestrians -- leaping over luggage--

Maximilian on his heels--

The Station Inspector follows relentlessly--

Insane whirlwind momentum as the station zips past--

Hugo pants for air, glancing back in panic--

Maximilian is closer and closer--

The Station Inspector spiders after them -- his leg brace
screeching --

Hugo speeds into a CAFE--

5   INT. TRAIN STATION -- CAFE - DAY   5

Hugo agilely weaves between the little tables and the sniffy
French waiters -- around dancers and a little dance band--

Maximilian follows, not quite so agilely, upsetting tables
and waiters--

Chaos--!

MADAME EMILIE, the shy older woman who runs the cafe, screams
and clutches her beloved little DACHSHUND to her chest--

The dachshund barks furiously at Maximilian--

Hugo zooms out of the cafe--

6   INT. TRAIN STATION -- GRAND HALL - DAY   6

Hugo loops around an outside table--

Where a man who looks suspiciously like James Joyce is having
a demitasse with a man who looks suspiciously like Salvador
Dali--

They are agog as Hugo races around them ... followed by
Maximilian ... followed by the Station Inspector--

Hugo finally sprints away from the cafe.

The Station Inspector calls after him:

                    STATION INSPECTOR
              STOP THAT CHILD! -- APPREHEND!

MONSIEUR FRICK, the shy older gentleman who runs a NEWSPAPER
KIOSK across from the cafe, makes a half-hearted grab for
Hugo--

But Hugo suddenly--

Dives--

Sliding on the polished floor between Monsieur Frick's legs--

Then he's up and gone--

Monsieur Frick looks up, alarmed, leaps to the side as--

Maximilian thunders past--

The Station Inspector follows--

Then Hugo sees his chance to escape!

He can see that a TRAIN is about to pull into the station at
one of the platforms.

He diverts in that direction, running flat out -- leaping
over luggage -- his wake sending newspapers flying--

6A   INT. TRAIN STATION -- PLATFORM - DAY   6A

He zips past a PLATFORM GATE and guard -- just like a city
kid jumping the turnstiles on the subway--

                                                      (CONTINUED)

Ahead of him, the train is slowing, almost pulling up to the platform. Passengers are waiting to board.

Hugo starts running along the long platform--

Maximilian and the Station Inspector right behind him--

But--

The platform ends in a SPIKED IRON FENCE.

Hugo is going to be trapped!

The train is almost up to the platform now--

The dog and the Station Inspector bear down on Hugo--

Hugo sees the dead end ahead--

And makes his move--

At the last possible second--

He leaps up to the wrought iron girders that knit over the tracks like ribs--

Scales them like a monkey--

Swinging and scaling over the tracks--

Just as the train pulls in right below him--

It rumbles beneath him.

Hugo leaps down to the platform on the other side--

The Station Inspector and Maximilian are trapped on the other side of the train.

Hugo disappears into a crowd. Gone.

On the other side of the train, the annoyed Station Inspector is enveloped in a disorienting cloud of steam--

He accidentally knocks into a MATRONLY GERMAN TOURIST -- his leg brace catches on her dress -- she bellows in German -- the discombobulated Station Inspector stumbles over a cart of baggage--

[Or similar moment of comic frustration.]

6A   CONTINUED: 6A

He's thwarted again.

7   OMITTED   7

8   INT. TRAIN STATION -- TUNNELS - DAY   8

Hugo weaves through the tunnels.

Comes to an iron door and enters...

9   INT. TRAIN STATION -- SECRET APARTMENT - DAY   9

It is like stepping into the heart of a mechanical toy.

Wheels and gears hang everywhere. There are rows of jars
filled with cogs, screws and bits of toys. Tools. Scavenged
furniture.

Hugo's home and makeshift workshop.

He sits on a battered old trunk for a moment. Disheartened.

He pulls out a large POCKET WATCH. Looks at it.

Takes a deep breath.

Time to go to work.

He picks up a bucket of heavy tools and goes.

10   INT. TRAIN STATION -- TUNNELS - DAY   10

Huge moves through the tunnels.

Stops behind a large clock. He can see the station through
the clock face. He checks the time on his pocket watch.

Then he uses tools from the bucket to wind the clock's
mechanism.

Then he continues on.

Opens a hatch and climbs down a rickety ladder...

11   INT. TRAIN STATION -- HANGING CLOCK - DAY   11

He climbs down <u>into</u> a large clock that is suspended from the
ceiling of the Grand Hall. Clock dials and intricate works
surround him on all four sides.

While he winds all four clockworks, he looks out into the
station below...

He sees Madame Emilie, the shy older woman who runs the cafe,
cooing to her little dachshund.

He sees Monsieur Frick, the shy older gentleman who runs the
newspaper kiosk, watching her.

Monsieur Frick summons up his nerve. Timidly approaches her.
Bows rather formally. She is delighted. He tries to pet the
dachshund. The dog snaps at him. Madame Emilie is mortified.
Monsieur Frick retreats.

Hugo climbs up, out of the clock...

12   INT. TRAIN STATION -- BASE OF TOWER STAIRS - DAY   12

Hugo continues on.

He approaches the Tower Stairs.

13   OMITTED   13

14   INT. TRAIN STATION -- TOWER STAIRS - DAY   14

Hugo climbs and climbs and climbs. His bucket of tools is
heavy.

An endless staircase inside a high tower.

15   INT. TRAIN STATION -- CLOCK TOWER - DAY   15

Hugo emerges at the very top of the station.

An enormous clock. The motors and gears of the mechanism are
huge, bigger than he is. Hugo puts a crank into the works and
uses all his strength to turn it.

15   CONTINUED: 15

It is like something out of METROPOLIS.

And beyond the clock...

Paris.

A panoramic view.

Somewhat unreal.

Like an exquisite toy model.

Exhausted, Hugo finally completes winding the clock.

He takes a moment to look over the majestic city.

And we fade to...

16   INT. TRAIN STATION -- TOY BOOTH - EVENING   16

The Grand Hall is almost empty.

Georges, in his hat and coat, is closing up the shop. Pulling
down a heavy grate.

Hugo stands silently behind him.

                    GEORGES
                (not turning)
          I know you're there ... What's
          your name, boy?

                    HUGO
          Hugo ... Hugo Cabret.

                    GEORGES
          Stay away from me, Hugo Cabret,
          or I'll drag you to the Station
          Inspector's office and he'll
          lock you up in his little cell
          and you'll never get out and
          you'll never go to school and
          you'll never get married and
          have children of your own to
          take things that don't belong to
          them.

Georges completes locking the gate and goes.

                                                          (CONTINUED)

16   CONTINUED: 16

Hugo follows.

They walk through the echoing station.

> HUGO
> Give me back my notebook.

> GEORGES
> I am going home to <u>burn</u> your notebook.

Georges sweeps through the doors, leaving the station.

Hugo stops at the doors, hesitates for a moment.

He is extremely uncomfortable at the idea of leaving the
station. It has become his whole world. Everything beyond is
threatening.

But his need now is great. He steels himself, takes a breath
and pushes through the doors, following Georges.

17   EXT. STREETS - EVENING   17

Georges walks through the dark streets of Paris.

Hugo follows.

It is the spirit of the great city we see, not the real
thing. Shapes and silhouettes of buildings. Architectural
details. Sounds. Illusion.

Like a lovingly crafted 1930's movie set.

> HUGO
> You can't burn my notebook.

> GEORGES
> And who's to stop me?

Hugo wasn't prepared for leaving the station. It's cold. He
has no winter coat. He pulls his clothes tightly around him.

Later...

Georges walks on.

Hugo follows. A little closer.

Later...

17   CONTINUED: 17

Georges walks under a street lamp.

Hugo follows. A little closer still.

Later...

Georges walks over a bridge.

Hugo follows. A little closer still.

Later...

Georges moves through a sinister alley.

Hugo, scared, is walking right next to him now.

Georges ignores him.

Snow begins to fall.

18   EXT. GRAVEYARD - NIGHT   18

Georges and Hugo walk through a graveyard.

Twisted trees. The shape of tombstones. Like Lean's GREAT
EXPECTATIONS.

Snow continues to fall.

19   EXT. APARTMENT BUILDING - NIGHT   19

Georges walks to a decrepit apartment building. Right across
from the graveyard. Shabby part of town.

The old man stops and unlocks the chipped front door with a
large key.

Hugo waits.

Georges enters the building and, without a glance, slams the
door shut behind him.

Hugo stands there.

Snow falls.

Hugo steps back, studies the building.

19   CONTINUED: 19

He sees Georges enter an upper floor apartment. Sees a handsome older woman -- his wife -- greet him. They disappear from view.

Huge scans the other windows. He sees Isabelle, the girl from the Toy Booth, in another room of the apartment.

She is reading by the window.

Hugo watches her.

Snow collects on his head.

He finally tosses a pebble up at the window. Isabelle looks down. Sees him.

She stares at him quizzically.

He motions for her to come down.

She is intrigued but unsure.

He motions. Begs. Please.

Isabelle smiles.

She loves nothing more than an adventure.

She disappears from the window.

20   EXT. GRAVEYARD - NIGHT   20

Hugo stands shivering.

Isabelle runs to him.

                    ISABELLE
          Who are you?

                    HUGO
          Your grandfather stole my
          notebook. I need to get it back
          before he burns it.

                    ISABELLE
          Papa Georges isn't my
          grandfather and he isn't a
          thief!

                                              (CONTINUED)

> He told me all about you, young
> gentleman. You're nothing but a
> ... a <u>reprobate</u>!

She is delighted with the word. He doesn't understand.

> HUGO
> Can you help me get inside?

> ISABELLE
> No. You have to go.

> HUGO
> Not without my notebook--

> ISABELLE
> Why do you need it so badly?

> HUGO
> (hesitates)
> I ... I can't tell you.

> ISABELLE
> Is it a secret?!

> HUGO
> Yes.

> ISABELLE
> Good! I love secrets! Tell me this instant!

> HUGO
> No!

> ISABELLE
> If you won't tell me you have to go.

> HUGO
> Not without--

> ISABELLE
> I'll get in trouble. Just go home!

He won't budge.

> ISABELLE
> All right! I'll make sure he
> doesn't burn your notebook.

He looks at her.

20   CONTINUED: 20

                              ISABELLE
                    Trust me.

He looks at her.

He nods.

He runs off.

She watches him go.

What a strange boy.

She smiles.

21   INT. TRAIN STATION -- SECRET APARTMENT - NIGHT   21

Hugo enters. Still cold.

He strikes a match. Lights a few candles.

A golden glow fills the strange chamber.

Hugo takes out his pocket watch and hangs it on a special
hook by the bed.

Then he moves to a corner...

There is something covered in an old sheet...

He pulls off the sheet to reveal...

The AUTOMATON.

An amazing mechanical man. A couple feet tall. Exposed gears
and levers. Clockworks and springs. In a state of disrepair.
We recognize the strange, haunting face from the drawings in
Hugo's notebook.

The Automaton sits at a little desk. Pen poised to write
something.

Hugo stares at the passive face of the Automaton.

And remembers.

                         HUGO (V.O.)
                    What is it...?

21   CONTINUED: 21

                           HUGO'S FATHER (V.O.)
                    It's called an Automaton.

The <u>color fades</u> as we go six months back in time...

22   INT. FLASHBACK -- CABRET APARTMENT - NIGHT   22

Hugo and his <u>FATHER</u> live in a poor, cramped garret. Big
skylight. Paris beyond. An enormous full moon beyond that.

The Automaton -- now in much worse condition, battered and
rusty, missing parts -- sits before Hugo and his Father.

                           HUGO
                    An <u>Automaton</u>...

                           HUGO'S FATHER
                    I found him abandoned in the attic of the museum.

                           HUGO
                    What does he do?

                           HUGO'S FATHER
                       (tinkering with it)
                    He's a windup figure, like a music
                    box ... This is the most
                    complicated one I've ever seen by
                    far. You see? This one can <u>write</u>.

                           HUGO
                       (transfixed)
                    Who built him?

                           HUGO'S FATHER
                    I would think a magician.

                           HUGO
                    A magician!

                           HUGO'S FATHER
                    That's right. Magicians used
                    machines like this when I was a
                    boy... And the best ones were made
                    in London.

                           HUGO
                    Where mother was from?

                                                        (CONTINUED)

22   CONTINUED: 22

                    HUGO'S FATHER
          She was from Coventry, moved to
          London later... But no one could
          figure out how they danced or
          walked or sang. But the secret was
          always in the clockwork.

                    HUGO
          Can we fix it?!

                    HUGO'S FATHER
          Oh, I don't know, Hugo, it's
          awfully rusted and finding the
          parts would be...

He sees Hugo's disappointment.

                    HUGO'S FATHER
          Of course we can fix it! We're
          clock makers, aren't we! ... But
          only when I've gotten through all
          my work at the shop and at the
          museum, you understand?

Hugo hugs him. His father smiles.

The Automaton seems to watch them.

23   INT. FLASHBACK -- CLOCK SHOP - DAY   23

Music.

Hugo sweeps up as his father works fixing clocks.

The tiny, cramped shop is a jumble of clocks, watches, gears,
movements, springs, dials.

24   INT. FLASHBACK -- MUSEUM - EVENING   24

Music.

Hugo's father winds and oils clocks in an old museum filled
with Victorian curiosities.

25   INT. FLASHBACK -- CABRET APARTMENT - NIGHT   25

Music.

25   CONTINUED: 25

Hugo and his father work on the Automaton together. They
huddle at the workbench.

Hugo's father patiently teaches him. Hugo learns eagerly.

Hugo's father smiles and points out a very unique HEART-
SHAPED KEYHOLE at the back of the Automaton:

                    HUGO'S FATHER
          You see this keyhole? Another
          complication. Another mystery...

                    HUGO
          That makes you happy.

                    HUGO'S FATHER
          Everything that makes it unique is
          a clue to the person who built
          it... A keyhole that's shaped like
          a heart? That means something...
          But unfortunately we don't have the
          key.

Hugo's father stops to make a note: drawing a unique heart-
shaped key that will fit the keyhole.

We realize he is writing in the NOTEBOOK, the one Georges
took.

26   INT. FLASHBACK -- MUSEUM - NIGHT   26

Music.

Hugo's father is working on a stubborn clock at the museum.

Then...

The music stops...

Hugo's father slowly turns...

Curious...

He moves to a stairway...

Looks down...

He sees...

(CONTINUED)

26   CONTINUED: 26

A PILLAR OF FLAME.

Raging right up at him.

27   INT. FLASHBACK -- CABRET APARTMENT - NIGHT   27

It is very late.

Hugo is working on the Automaton.

The door opens.

He turns eagerly:

                    HUGO
          I fixed the gears in the--

But it is not his father.

It is his UNCLE CLAUDE. Unshaven. Greasy. Crude. Huge.

                    HUGO
          Uncle Claude...?

                    UNCLE CLAUDE
          There was a fire. Your father's
          dead. Pack your things quickly.
          You're coming with me.

Hugo stares.

28   EXT. FLASHBACK -- STREETS - NIGHT   28

Hugo lugs the heavy Automaton, covered in a sheet, as he
follows Uncle Claude through the empty streets.

Hugo struggles to keep up with Uncle Claude's huge gait.

                    UNCLE CLAUDE
          You'll be my apprentice. You'll
          live with me and I'll show you how
          to take care of them clocks.
               (Takes a swig from a flask)
          I'm getting too old to be climbing
          through them tunnels.

They turn a corner.

                                                    (CONTINUED)

28   CONTINUED: 28

And ahead of them...

The Train Station.

29   INT. FLASHBACK -- TRAIN STATION -- APARTMENT - NIGHT   29

Uncle Claude and Hugo enter the secret apartment. It is
filthy and rank. Dickensian.

Hugo sets down the Automaton. Looks around.

                    UNCLE CLAUDE
               They built these apartments for them who ran the
               station, years ago. Everyone's forgotten they're
               here. You sleep in the corner.

Uncle Claude plops down. Drinks.

                    UNCLE CLAUDE
               Get some sleep. We start work at five.

                    HUGO
               What about school?

                    UNCLE CLAUDE
               You're finished with school. There
               won't be time for that once you're
               in them walls ... You should thank
               me.

Uncle Claude clears his throat. Takes a drink. Looks away.

Hugo carries the Automaton to his corner.

He sits.

Dazed.

Absolutely forlorn.

Then he pulls the sheet off the Automaton.

He looks into the Automaton's face.

His only friend.

They sit together.

30   OMITTED   30

31   INT. TRAIN STATION -- APARTMENT - NIGHT   31

Hugo sits, looking at the Automaton.

Alone. Despondent.

We fade to...

32   INT. TRAIN STATION -- GRAND HALL - MORNING   32

Hugo peers out from behind an air vent.

Waiting. Watching.

Madame Emilie is opening her little cafe. Her dachshund
hovers protectively.

Monsieur Frick approaches cautiously. Bows gallantly and
offers her a newspaper from his kiosk. Madame Emilie is
charmed. The dachshund attacks this time! It chases Monsieur
Frick away. Madame Emilie follows in horror.

Hugo seizes his opportunity--

He scrambles quickly from the air vent--

Races to the cafe--

Grabs a croissant and bottle of milk--

Runs off--

Disappearing into the crowd of morning commuters.

33   INT. TRAIN STATION -- GRAND HALL - MORNING   33

Hugo moves through the grown up world, eating the croissant.
No one notices him.

He heads towards the stairs -- not realizing that the Station
Inspector is heading down the stairs!

Cut to--

33   CONTINUED: 33

The Station Inspector stops on the stairs. Looks around.

We realize that Hugo is hiding behind a column right by the Inspector.

But the Station Inspector is distracted by the sight of LISETTE, a beautiful and shy girl who runs a little flower stall. She's pushing a cart of vibrant flowers through the terminal.

The Station Inspector finally continues down the stairs. Hugo slips away.

The Station Inspector gazes at Lisette. He's besotted, has been for a while.

He gets up his nerve ... Compulsively straightens the buttons on his uniform ... Puts on an awkward smile ... He begins to approach...

But then his leg braces squeaks sharply. It echoes through the terminal. He stops. Embarrassed.

He gives up. Moves off.

34   INT. TRAIN STATION -- TOY BOOTH - MORNING   34

Georges is opening the Toy Booth.

Hugo stands silently behind him.

                    GEORGES
          I thought I might see you today.

                    HUGO
          I need my notebook.

                    GEORGES
          Why do you need it so badly?

                    HUGO
          To help me ... fix something.

                    GEORGES
          What?

Hugo doesn't answer.

(CONTINUED)

34   CONTINUED: 34

Georges hands Hugo a handkerchief tied up into a bundle. Hugo unties it.

Ashes. It is filled with ashes. Burned paper.

Hugo looks at the ashes. Horror and disbelief. Tears sting his eyes.

He can't breathe.

The ashes fall...

Cascade and swirl delicately down...

Over Hugo's shoes...

To the floor.

Hugo looks up at Georges.

He is shocked to see there are tears in <u>Georges'</u> eyes as well.

                    GEORGES
        Go away ... Please just go away.

Hugo wipes his eyes with his dirty, ashen hands, leaving long black smudges on his face.

He backs away.

Then he turns and runs off. Tears flowing freely now.

He races around a corner and--

35   INT. TRAIN STATION -- GRAND HALL - MORNING   35

--Bang!

He runs right into Isabelle. She was hiding, waiting for him.

                  ISABELLE
      Hey!

                  HUGO
     Sorry -- I--

                  ISABELLE
    I saw. Are you crying?

                                      (CONTINUED)

35   CONTINUED: 35

                          HUGO
                    No!

                          ISABELLE
                    Hold still.

She uses her handkerchief to dry his eyes and clean his face
as:

                          ISABELLE
                    There's nothing wrong with crying.
                    Sidney Carton cries. And Heathcliff
                    too. In books they're crying all the
                    time.

                          HUGO
                       (grabs handkerchief)
                    I can do it!

                          ISABELLE
                    I have to talk to you. It's terribly
                    important. But not here. We're too
                    ... exposed.

She dramatically grabs his hand and pulls him off.

36   INT. TRAIN STATION -- GRAND HALL - MORNING   36

Hugo continues to clean his face as they move through a
different part of the station. Isabelle is carrying a book.

                          HUGO
                    Where are we going?

                          ISABELLE
                    Only to the most wonderful place on
                    earth! Neverland and Oz and
                    Treasure Island all wrapped up into
                    one.

Ahead of them...

Her secret realm ...

37   INT. TRAIN STATION -- BOOKSTORE - MORNING   37

A little bell jangles when they enter.

                                                            (CONTINUED)

<u>MONSIEUR LABISSE</u>, the shop owner, is perched high on a stool
at the front of the store like the Caterpillar from ALICE IN
WONDERLAND, peering over a stack of dusty books.

He is a tall, stern man. He brightens when he sees Isabelle.
But he is extremely suspicious of Hugo.

> ISABELLE
> Good morning, Monsieur Labisse, may I present
> Monsieur Hugo Cabret, a very old and dear boon
> companion.

> MONSIEUR LABISSE
> (bows)
> Monsieur Cabret.

> HUGO
> Hello.

> ISABELLE
> (handing him book)
> Thank you for this. I think I'm
> halfway in love with David
> Copperfield ... Photography?

> MONSIEUR LABISSE
> (points)
> Back corner left, top shelf.

> ISABELLE
> Thank you.

Monsieur Labisse watches them go. Hugo's dirty clothes and
long hair convince him he must be a shoplifter -- or worse.

Isabelle leads Hugo deeper into the store.

It is a world of books. Stacked in every direction. To the
ceiling. Rivers of books. Mountains of books. Gloriously
cluttered.

> HUGO
> Listen, what's so important?

> ISABELLE
> Papa Georges still has your notebook.
> He didn't burn it. That was all a
> trick.

(CONTINUED)

> HUGO

Why?

She climbs a ladder in search of a book:

> ISABELLE

I don't know. The notebook made him very upset. He and Mama Jeanne stayed up late talking about it. I think he was crying.

Hugo thinks about this. How strange.

> HUGO

It's a mystery.

> ISABELLE

I know!

> HUGO

Why are you helping me?

> ISABELLE

Because this might be an <u>adventure</u>! I've never had one, outside of books.

She grabs a book. Comes back down the ladder.

> ISABELLE

I think we should be very ... <u>clandestine</u>.

> HUGO

Okay.

> ISABELLE

By the way, my name's Isabelle ... Do you want a book? Monsieur Labisse lets me borrow them. I could get one for you.

> HUGO

No.

> ISABELLE
> (horrified)

Don't you like books?!

> HUGO

No, I do ... My father and I used to read Jules Verne together...

(CONTINUED)

37   CONTINUED: 37

He stops.

She senses his strong emotion. Respects it.

They move to Monsieur Labisse at the front counter.

                        ISABELLE
                    (re: book)
                May I?

                    MONSIEUR LABISSE
            Of course. Good day, Isabelle.

Monsieur Labisse watches Hugo with suspicion as they leave
the shop.

38   INT. TRAIN STATION -- GRAND HALL - MORNING   38

They move through the bustling station.

                        HUGO
            How do I get my notebook back?

                        ISABELLE
            I think you should stand up to him.
            He'll respect that ... Don't tell
            him we talked. I'll help you if I
            can ... Be steadfast!

She disappears into the crowd.

He watches her go.

Be steadfast? What a peculiar girl.

39   INT. TRAIN STATION -- TOY BOOTH - DAY   39

Georges is sitting at the counter. Evenly staring at
something.

He aimlessly cuts and re-cuts a deck of cards with one hand
as he stares.

We finally see what he is staring at...

Hugo stands there on the other side of the counter. Staring
back at him. Steadfast.

                                                          (CONTINUED)

It is like a showdown.

Finally:

>   HUGO
>   I don't believe you burned my notebook.

>   GEORGES
>   You don't? ... Well, maybe I did and
>   maybe I didn't. You'll never know,
>   will you?

Hugo holds his ground.

>   GEORGES
>   Shall I call the Station Inspector?

Hugo holds his ground.

>   GEORGES
>   Go ... away.

Hugo holds his ground.

Georges glares at him.

Hugo glares back.

A long beat.

Gunfighters.

Neither blinks.

Then...

Georges slowly reaches under the counter...

He pulls something out...

Something covered in a handkerchief...

He sets it on the counter...

With the panache of a magician, he pulls off the handkerchief
to reveal...

The toy mouse that Hugo broke earlier.

                         GEORGES
                    Fix it.

Hugo looks at him.

                         GEORGES
                    I said, fix it.

                         HUGO
                    I need my tools.

Georges pulls out a canister of tiny screwdrivers, pliers,
files and hammers.

                         GEORGES
                    I know you've been stealing parts from the shop ...
                    Might as well use those you haven't stolen yet.

Hugo looks at the broken toy mouse. Then at Georges.

                         HUGO
                    If I fix it, do I get my notebook?

                         GEORGES
                    We'll see.

A challenge.

Hugo starts to work.

He uses the tiny tools ... hammering ... screwing ...
adjusting ... tinkering...

Georges watches.

Hugo fixes the spring ... fits the key ... hammers the
body...

Finally he sets the toy mouse down on the counter.

Georges looks at it.

He winds it.

The toy mouse skitters playfully across the counter.

Georges is impressed, tries not to show it.

                         HUGO
                    Give me my notebook.

>   GEORGES
>   You've got a bit of talent. But
>   you'll have to prove there's more to
>   you than being a thief ... You can
>   earn your notebook.

>   HUGO
>   How?

>   GEORGES
>   Come to the booth everyday. I'll
>   decide how long you must work for
>   each item you stole, and it will be
>   up to me to decide when you have
>   earned your notebook, if ever.

>   HUGO
>   I already have a job.

>   GEORGES
>   Thief is not a job, boy.

>   HUGO
>   I have another job, but I'll come when I can.

>   GEORGES
>   You begin tomorrow. Go away.

>   HUGO
>   I'll begin now.

Hugo bravely goes into the booth and gets a broom.

Starts sweeping up.

Georges watches him.

Across the station, a little DANCE BAND is starting up at Madame Emilie's cafe.

A few couples dance.

An afternoon tea dance.

A lovely, bygone image. Couples dancing under the massive iron ribs of the great train station.

The music echoes throughout the Grand Hall.

The music from the band takes us to...

40   INT./EXT. - <u>MONTAGE</u> - DAY/NIGHT   40

Dance band music as...

... Georges does a card trick. Hugo watches the trick closely. Georges notices.

... Georges teaches Hugo how to do the card trick.

... Hugo demonstrates the card trick to the Automaton.

... Hugo watches from the toy booth as Isabelle and two of her SCHOOL FRIENDS playfully dance to the dance band. He watches them laughing together... Hugo notices a cog, spring or gear in the trash. He takes it.

... Late Night. Hugo works on the Automaton. Intensely focused. Sweat on his brow. He tries to use the little cog or gear he got from the trash to fix the Automaton. He has to get it to work!

...Night. Hugo stands in the graveyard outside the Melies apartment, watching the family through the windows. He's like a statue, just watching. Snow has accumulated on his shoulders and shoes.

...Hugo works on the Automaton. It looks almost done now: polished, cleaned, beautiful and ready. But for one thing. Hugo is trying various keys and bits of metal in a HEART-SHAPED KEYHOLE in the Automaton's back. Nothing works.

He faces the Automaton.

                    HUGO
          Where is it...? Where's the key...?

The Automaton looks at him. Hugo sighs.

...Late night. The station is closed and deserted. From high above we see Hugo crossing the Grand Hall. A tiny figure in the vast chamber.

...Late night. Hugo roots through a trash can by the cafe. Finds some food.

...Late night. Hugo sits alone. Intensely staring at the Automaton. How can he get it to work?

The montage ends.

41   INT. TRAIN STATION -- GRAND HALL - DAY   41

Hugo is waiting for Isabelle outside the book shop.

He sees the Station Inspector and Maximilian cutting through
the crowd. Hugo ducks around a corner and watches nervously.

But the Station Inspector has another quarry today.

A young STREET KID, around Hugo's age, is loitering near
another shop.

The Station Inspector stalks him and then sweeps down like a
bird of prey. The Street Kid makes a move to bolt--

But the Station Inspector releases Maximilian, who leaps,
crouches and snarls in front of the terrified Kid--

The Station Inspector grabs the Kid brutally. Shakes him.

                    STATION INSPECTOR
          Where are your designated adults?!
          Answer me!

                    STREET KID
               (terrified)
          Got none.

Without another word, the Station Inspector begins to drag
him   away--

But then his leg brace locks awkwardly--

                    STATION INSPECTOR
          Vexation!

He stiff-legs off, dragging the kid with him. Maximilian
lopes after them.

Hugo darts into an air vent.

42   INT. TRAIN STATION - NARROW PASSAGE/INSPECTOR'S OFFICE -DAY 42

Hugo is in a cramped passage that overlooks the Station
Inspector's office, peering through a clock face.

                                                    (CONTINUED)

42   CONTINUED: 42

The Station Inspector's office is like the man himself:
compulsively neat and organized to within an inch of its
life. Strangely, there is a FIRE POLE in the corner that
disappears through a trap door.

The Street Kid is in a tiny, awful CELL. He is sobbing.
Maximilian sits alert, glaring in at the Kid.

The Station Inspector is trying to repair his leg brace as he
talks on the phone:

                    STATION INSPECTOR
                 (on phone)
             ... yes, another one. Useless waste
             of an orphan by the looks of it,
             bedraggled in the extreme...
                 (turns away, almost as
                  if not to offend the
                  kid)
             A bit licey I should think.

Suddenly--

Maximilian turns. Looks toward Hugo, ears perked.

Hugo sinks back into the darkness.

43   INT./EXT. TRAIN STATION/TUNNELS -- DAY   43

Watching through a grill (at pavement level), Hugo sees the
Station Inspector dragging the Street Kid through the doors
of the station and throwing him into a POLICE TRUCK.

Inside are some other ORPHANS. Heads shaved like prisoners.
Horrible. The truck roars off.

The Station Inspector comes back inside.

He stands looking over his domain. Maximilian at his side.
Imperious.

Hugo disappears back into the tunnels.

44   INT. TRAIN STATION -- BOOKSTORE - DAY   44

Hugo and Isabelle move through the bookstore.

                                                        (CONTINUED)

                         ISABELLE
               ... I'm still looking for your
               notebook. I have to be very
               circumspect.

She loves the word.

                         HUGO
               You better not look inside.

                         ISABELLE
               If I find it I should be able to
               look inside it.

                         HUGO
               Then don't look for it!

                         ISABELLE
               I'm trying to help. Why are you
               being so mean?

To Hugo she suddenly looks very grown up. She is disappointed
in him. His heart sinks.

                         HUGO
               Just ... Promise me you won't open it.

                         ISABELLE
               Fine.

They wander deeper into the store.

Monsieur Labisse, perched on his high stool, keeps an wary
eye on Hugo.

Hugo picks up a French copy of ROBIN HOOD (ROBIN HOOD LE
PROSCRIT), smiles.

                         HUGO
               I saw this movie! With Douglas Fairbanks. Did you
               see that?

                         ISABELLE
               I've never seen a movie.

                         HUGO
               What?!

                         ISABELLE
               Isn't it appalling?!

                                                        (CONTINUED)

44   CONTINUED: 44

                         HUGO
              You've never seen a movie? <u>Not</u> <u>ever</u>?

                         ISABELLE
              Papa Georges won't let me. He's
              very strict about it.

                         HUGO
                    (excited)
              I love movies! My father always took me
              for my birthday.

Hugo is surprised he suddenly spoke about his father. He does
not regret it though.

They wander through the teetering piles of books in silence.

                         ISABELLE
              Is your father dead?

                         HUGO
              I don't want to talk about it.

A beat.

She takes his hand for a quick moment, then releases it.

A gesture of support. Friendship.

They continue strolling.

Hugo stops. An idea. He looks at her.

                         HUGO
              Isabelle ... Do you want to have an
              adventure?

Her eyes light up.

45   EXT. MOVIE THEATRE - DAY   45

Again, the suggestion of Paris.

A movie theatre facade. An Art Deco marquee. A green neon
sign: Silent Movie Festival.

Isabelle and Hugo stand looking up at the theatre.

She looks at him. Beams.

45   CONTINUED: 45

He nods his head and nonchalantly leads her down an alley
next to the theatre...

46   EXT. ALLEY NEXT TO THEATRE - DAY   46

They move down the alley ... passing a series of fading movie
posters ... Keaton ... Lon Chaney ... Doug Fairbanks...

He stops at a side door and begins to deftly pick the lock
with one of his tools.

                    ISABELLE
          We could get into trouble.

                    HUGO
          That's how you know it's an adventure.

Click.

He opens the door and peeks in. Coast is clear.

He looks at her.

Yes or no?

She's game.

They sneak in.

47   INT. MOVIE THEATRE - DAY   47

The flickering light above.

The glowing screen.

Iridescent.

Hugo and Isabelle are sitting at the back.

The famous Harold Lloyd film SAFETY LAST is playing.

Isabelle's eyes are wide.

She's transported.

The magic of motion pictures.

                                                        (CONTINUED)

She's never seen one before. Life captured on the screen. Living, moving history.

The iridescent glow from the screen illuminates her face.

Hugo glances to her.

Her enchantment touches him.

He smiles.

The light flickers above them.

Time passes...

It's the climax of SAFETY LAST.

Isabelle is wrapped up in the movie.

Can barely watch.

Can barely breathe.

Harold Lloyd is climbing dangerously around the outside of the skyscraper. Acrobatic stunts still hair-raising after all these years. Harold Lloyd grabs the big clock face. It springs open--!

Isabelle grabs Hugo's arm in horror--!

Hugo looks at her. Amused.

Harold Lloyd clings to the hands of the clock and then continues to climb around the building.

Then...

From the darkness behind Hugo and Isabelle...

Two huge white hands slowly descend...

Like the Frankenstein Monster's mitts...

Grabbing them on the shoulder...

They jump!

The THEATRE MANAGER looms over them.

47   CONTINUED: 47

                         THEATRE MANAGER
                    How did you two rats get in here?!

48   EXT. MOVIE THEATRE - DAY   48

The Manager dumps them outside.

                         THEATRE MANAGER
                    And I better not see you in here again!

He closes the doors.

Hugo and Isabelle laugh and run off.

49   EXT. BANK OF THE SEINE - DAY   49

It is chilly. Fog.

Hugo and Isabelle walk home along the Seine.

The silhouette of bridges. The sound of lapping water. The
shape of boats moving past. Radio music from a houseboat.

Hugo tightrope walks along the edge of the bank, like Harold
Lloyd on a ledge from SAFETY LAST.

                         HUGO
                    Why doesn't Papa Georges let you go
                    to the movies?

                         ISABELLE
                    I don't know. He never said. I bet
                    my parents would have let me. I'm
                    sure they were very aesthetic.

                         HUGO
                    What happened to them?

                         ISABELLE
                    They died when I was a baby. Papa
                    Georges and Mama Jeanne are my
                    godparents, so they took me in.
                    They're very nice about most
                    everything, except the movies.

                         HUGO
                    My father took me to the movies all
                    the time.

We saw Tom Mix and Lon Chaney. But
Douglas Fairbanks was my favorite.

Hugo sword fights along the bank for a moment.

A beat as they walk.

                    ISABELLE
          What was he like?

                    HUGO
          He loved the movies ... Ever since
          he was a kid and the movies were
          new. He told me about the first one
          he ever saw. He went into a dark
          room and on a white screen he saw a
          rocket fly into the eye of the man
          in the moon.
               (smiles)
          He said it was like seeing his dreams
          in the middle of the day.

A beat as they walk. He speaks quietly.

                    HUGO
          The movies were our special place. It
          was just us ... We'd go in and watch
          something ... and for a little while we
          didn't miss my mom so much.

She's touched by his honesty.

                    ISABELLE
          You think about him a lot.

                    HUGO
          All the time.

A beat as they walk.

                    ISABELLE
          Who looks after you?

                    HUGO
          My uncle was supposed to ... But he
          started going away a lot. Drinking.
          Staying out all night ... One day he
          didn't come back.

                    ISABELLE
          So you're all alone?

                                          (CONTINUED)

49   CONTINUED: 49

                         HUGO
                  Not completely.

A beat as they walk.

She stops.

                         ISABELLE
                  Hugo ... Where do you live?

He stops.

Looks at her.

Should he tell her?

Should he trust her?

Yes.

He points.

                         HUGO
                  There.

She looks...

Across the river...

The Train Station.

50   INT.. TRAIN STATION -- GRAND HALL - DAY   50

Hugo and Isabelle move through the crowd.

She is incredulous.

                         HUGO
                  ... My uncle taught me how to
                  run the clocks. So I just keep
                  on doing it ... Maybe he'll come
                  back one day, but I doubt it.

                         ISABELLE
                  But ... Aren't you afraid someone
                  will find out?

                                                              (CONTINUED)

50   CONTINUED: 50

> HUGO
> Not as long as the clocks keep on working and no
> one sees me.

> ISABELLE
> What do you do for money?

> HUGO
> Don't need any.

A beat as they walk.

> ISABELLE
> Can I see it?

> HUGO
> What?

> ISABELLE
> Where you live! In the walls.

> HUGO
> Maybe.

> ISABELLE
> Maybe?

Hugo suddenly sees...

The Station Inspector and Maximilian...

Walking right toward them...

> HUGO
> Act natural.

> ISABELLE
> What?

> HUGO
> Just keep walking. Act natural.

> ISABELLE
> (perplexed)
> How am I acting now?

Then she sees the Station Inspector and Maximilian.

She understands.

(CONTINUED)

CONTINUED: 50

Hugo grabs her cap and pulls it on, concealing his features a bit. They put on an elaborate show of "acting natural" as they walk toward the Station Inspector.

They pass him.

A sigh of relief.

But...

The Station Inspector stops.

Turns. His leg brace <u>squeaks</u> like a rifle shot.

                    STATION INSPECTOR
          Hey! You two.

Hugo and Isabelle freeze.

                    STATION INSPECTOR
          Come ... here.

Hugo is about to bolt.

Isabelle sees it in his eyes.

With a look, she cautions him against it.

She will handle this another way.

She drags him back to the Station Inspector. Puts on her sweetest face:

                    ISABELLE
          Good day, Monsieur!

                    STATION INSPECTOR
               (icy)
          Where are your parents?

                    ISABELLE
          I work with my Papa Georges at
          the Toy Booth, surely you've
          seen me there. And this is my
          cousin from the country, Hugo.
               (Whispers)
          You'll have to forgive him, he's a
          little simple-minded. Doltish,
          really. Poor thing.

The Station Inspector leans in.

Peers closely at Hugo.

Hugo gives him a simple-minded look.

Maximilian noses <u>right up to Hugo</u>.

Sniffing. A low growl.

> STATION INSPECTOR
> It seems Maximilian doesn't like the
> cut of your jib, little man ... Why
> would he dislike your jib?

> ISABELLE
> (to the rescue)
> Perhaps he smells my cat?! Christina
> Rossetti's her name, after the poetess!
> Would you like me to recite? "My heart
> is like a singing bird/Whose nest is in
> a watered shoot/My heart is like an
> apple tree/Whose boughs are bent with
> thickset fruit--!"

> STATION INSPECTOR
> All right, all right ... Go on then,
> but straight to your adult supervisors.
> This is a <u>treacherous</u> place, you
> understand? Locomotives.
> Machinery. Dismemberment...
> <u>Watch</u> <u>your</u> <u>step</u>.

He gives them a last chilling glare and goes.

They see him disappear into another part of the station.
They're free of him for the moment.

Hugo looks at Isabelle.

> HUGO
> Doltish?

> ISABELLE
> It worked didn't it?

They continue on.

(CONTINUED)

50   CONTINUED: 50

                         ISABELLE
              Now since I just saved your life how
              about letting me see your covert lair?

                         HUGO
              My what?

                         ISABELLE
              Where you live in the walls!

                         HUGO
              I can't understand what you're
              saying half the time.

                         ISABELLE
              That's because I am so gigantically literate.

                         HUGO
              I have to go now. I have things to
              do.

He walks. She follows.

                         ISABELLE
              Hold on! Where are you going? Now
              you've been to my home, isn't about
              time I saw yours? From what you
              told me, I am your only friend
              after all.

                         HUGO
              You're not my only friend.

His pace increases. She pursues him.

                         ISABELLE
              Being enigmatic doesn't suit you at
              all!

                         HUGO
              I've got to go. I should never have
              left the station to begin with!

Suddenly--

They find themselves in a great wave of people hurrying from
a train--

Too many big people pushing them back and forth, crowding
them, jostling them.

(CONTINUED)

Isabelle trips!

She falls.

Amidst the pounding crush of feet.

Scary.

Hugo turns.

His face.

Concern.

He pushes back.

Reaches for her.

His hand stretches out.

She takes his hand.

Her face.

Grateful.

He pulls her up to safety.

The crowd thins out around them.

But he is staring at something, amazed.

In the action, a necklace has emerged from her collar. A key
on a piece of string.

A distinctive heart-shaped key.

                    HUGO
          Where did you get that?!

                    ISABELLE
          None of your business.

She tucks the key away.

                    HUGO
          I need it.

                    ISABELLE
          What for?

                                        (CONTINUED)

50   CONTINUED: 50

                              HUGO
                    I just need it.

                              ISABELLE
                    Not unless you tell me why.

He looks at her.

50A   OMITTED   50A

50B   OMITTED   50B

50C   OMITTED   50C

51   OMITTED   51

52   OMITTED   52

53   INT. TRAIN STATION -- TUNNELS - DAY   53

Hugo leads her through the tunnels.

                              ISABELLE
                    This is marvelous! ... I feel like
                    Jean Valjean!

                              HUGO
                    I used to imagine I was the Phantom of
                    the Opera. Like in the movie.

                              ISABELLE
                    It was a book too. You know sometimes
                    things are books before they're movies!

He leads her through the iron door to...

54   INT.. TRAIN STATION -- SECRET APARTMENT - DAY   54

Hugo lights some candles.

She takes the apartment in. The cramped quarters. The chaos
of tools and machine parts hanging everywhere. She loves it!

                                                          (CONTINUED)

> ISABELLE
> Oh, this is superlative!

Hugo pulls a sheet off the Automaton.

She is instantly captivated by the wonderful machine.

> ISABELLE
> What is it?

> HUGO
> It's an automaton ... My father was fixing it
> before he died.

> ISABELLE
> Why would my key fit your father's machine?
> ... That doesn't make any sense.

They look at the Automaton for a moment.

> ISABELLE
> He looks sad.

> HUGO
> I think he's just waiting.

> ISABELLE
> For what?

> HUGO
> To work again. To do what he's supposed
> to do.

> ISABELLE
> What happens when you wind him up?

> HUGO
> I don't know.

She takes off her necklace.

Hands it to him.

He fills the Automaton's little inkwell with ink.

He puts a fresh piece of paper on the little writing desk.

It's ready.

Hugo pauses.

                              ISABELLE
                    What's the matter?

                              HUGO
                    I know it's silly but ... I think it's
                    going to be a message from my father.

                              ISABELLE
                    Do you want me to go?

He shakes his head.

A beat.

Then he carefully inserts the key.

And winds the Automaton.

Steps back.

The world hangs in suspense.

Nothing happens.

He looks at her.

She doesn't know what to say.

He looks back at the Automaton.

Nothing.

But...

Then we go...

INSIDE the Automaton's body:

Things begins to move...

A cascade of perfect movements, with hundreds of brilliantly
calibrated actions...

A spring connects to a series of gears...

The gears extend down to the base of the figure and turn
brass disks...

Two little hammers come down and trail along the edges of the
disks...

54   CONTINUED: 54

The little hammers translate motion back up through a series
of rods...

The rods silently turn other intricate mechanisms in the
figure's shoulder and neck...

The shoulder gears move...

Engaging the elbow...

Setting off a chain reaction of movements down to the
wrist...

And finally...

The hand.

OUTSIDE again:

Hugo and Isabelle watch.

The Automaton's hand moves slightly. Just a twitch.

They gasp.

Hugo and Isabelle lean forward, wide-eyed with wonder.

The miniature hand begins, very cautiously, to move.

Hugo and Isabelle hold their breath.

The Automaton dips the pen into the ink and begins to write.

It draws a small line. The hand moves. Another small line.
The hand moves. Another small line.

Hugo and Isabelle lean closer.

The Automaton continues to move. Dip the pen. Draw a line.
Move. Draw a line. Dip the pen. Move. Draw a line.

But it is meaningless.

A series of scratches and lines without order.

Nothing.

Hugo stares.

His heart sinking.

(CONTINUED)

Then the Automaton stops.

Finished.

Hugo is devastated.

> HUGO
> What an idiot -- Thinking I could fix it--

> ISABELLE
> Hugo--

> HUGO
> It's broken. It'll always be broken!

Anguish beyond tears.

She doesn't know what to do.

She goes to him. Trying to comfort.

> ISABELLE
> Hugo ... You can still--

> HUGO
> You don't understand. I thought if I
> could fix it ... I wouldn't be so alone.

He buries his head in his hands.

A long beat.

Then she notices something.

The Automaton is moving again.

> ISABELLE
> Hugo ... Hugo, look -- look!

He glances up.

> ISABELLE
> It's not done! It's not done!

They rush back to the Automaton.

It is moving more quickly now. All the gears and wheels
spinning perfectly. Draw-move-ink-draw-move.

Hugo realizes:

(CONTINUED)

                              HUGO
                    It's not writing ... It's <u>drawing</u>!

Indeed it is.

Faster and faster. A blur of ink. Lines forming together.
Shading and cross-hatching. Draw-move-draw-move-ink-draw-move-
draw.

An image begins to emerge.

We don't see it entirely.

We see bits and pieces. Something familiar about it.

Hugo and Isabelle stare.

Finally the Automaton <u>stops</u>.

It waits.

Pen poised.

Hugo and Isabelle exchange a glance.

And we finally see the image in full...

And recognize it instantly...

A TRIP TO THE MOON.

The round face of the man in the moon. Rocket protruding from
his right eye.

Hugo's father's favorite movie. The very image he told Hugo
about.

Hugo is trembling.

Suddenly--

The Automaton starts moving again--!

Hugo and Isabelle jump--!

The Automaton dips the pen and moves its hand into position.

And signs the drawing:

"Georges Melies."

(CONTINUED)

54   CONTINUED: 54

A flourish under the signature and then the Automaton is
done.

                    ISABELLE
          "Georges Melies" ... That's Papa
          Georges' name! Why did your father's
          machine sign Papa Georges' name?

                    HUGO
          I don't know...

                    ISABELLE
          And why does my key fit it?

Hugo shakes his head.

He just looks at the Automaton.

He smiles.

                    HUGO
          Thank you.

He turns to her.

                    HUGO
          It <u>was</u> a message from my father ...
          Now we have to figure it out.

She is delighted. A mystery!

55   EXT. APARTMENT BUILDING - EVENING   55

The sun is sinking.

Hugo and Isabelle approach the apartment building.

Hugo, who has watched it so often from outside, hesitates at
going in.

                    ISABELLE
          Come on.

They enter.

56   INT. APARTMENT - EVENING   56

Impoverished gentility.

A few small rooms. Neatly kept. Old furniture. Fading wallpaper.

MAMA JEANNE, Georges' wife, is sewing in a corner. She wears heavy reading glasses. She is a handsome older woman.

Isabelle and Hugo enter.

>   MAMA JEANNE
>   Isabelle...?

>   ISABELLE
>   (kisses her)
>   Mama Jeanne, we have to talk to you ...
>   This is Hugo Cabret.

>   HUGO
>   Good evening, ma'am.

>   MAMA JEANNE
>   Very good manners for a thief.

>   HUGO
>   I'm not a thief.

Jeanne considers him coolly over her glasses. Removes them.

>   MAMA JEANNE
>   What's going on, Isabelle?

>   ISABELLE
>   (excited)
>   Oh, well, it's a terribly long story,
>   filled with circumlocutions! It all
>   began several weeks ago when I was...

Hugo stops her:

>   HUGO
>   Wait.

He pulls something from inside his coat.

A piece of paper. Folded over.

He hands it to Mama Jeanne. She unfolds it.

It is the picture the Automaton drew. The image from A TRIP TO THE MOON.

(CONTINUED)

She stares down at it.

A complex range of emotions pass over her features ... shock
... nostalgia ... sadness ...

When she looks up at them there are tears in her eyes.

Isabelle is struck by the sight.

>   MAMA JEANNE
>   Children ... What have you done?

>   ISABELLE
>   Mama Jeanne...?

Mama Jeanne dries her eyes with a little handkerchief.

Isabelle finds there are tears in her eyes as well.

Hugo sees Isabelle's tears. Feels awful.

>   MAMA JEANNE
>   Where did you get it?

>   HUGO
>   You'll call me a liar.

>   MAMA JEANNE
>   No, child.

>   HUGO
>   A mechanical man drew it.

>   MAMA JEANNE
>   You have him?

>   HUGO
>   My father found him in a museum. No
>   one wanted him. We fixed him.

>   MAMA JEANNE
>   But it needed ...
>   (She realizes. Looks at Isabelle.)
>   My key.

Isabelle removes the key.

>   MAMA JEANNE
>   The key I gave you...

A beat as it all sinks in.

Then she stands.

She hands the drawing back to Hugo.

                    MAMA JEANNE
          Please, take it away. We can't
          dredge up the past now. And
          whatever happens, don't let Papa
          Georges see it.

                    HUGO
          Please tell us what's going on!

She begins to lead Hugo to the door.

                    MAMA JEANNE
          It's no business of yours. You must
          forget all this.

Hugo stops. Holds his ground.

                    HUGO
          We worked hard to fix it, my father
          and me, and ... it's all I have
          left of him ... I need to know what
          it means.

A beat.

Mama Jeanne looks at him.

Moved by his passion and need.

She looks at him seriously. Speaks with great compassion.

                    MAMA JEANNE
          There are things you are too young to
          understand ... You should not yet
          know such sadness.

Then...

They hear someone climbing up the stairs to the apartment.

                    ISABELLE
          It's Papa Georges!

                                          (CONTINUED)

56   CONTINUED: 56

                    MAMA JEANNE
          He can't know you're here. This way...

She quickly leads them through the apartment to the master
bedroom...

57   INT. APARTMENT -- MASTER BEDROOM - EVENING   57

Mama Jeanne hurries them in:

                    MAMA JEANNE
          Just keep quiet. I'll find a way to
          get him out of the apartment. Not a
          noise from either of you.

She inadvertently glances toward a large armoire. Hugo and
Isabelle both notice.

Then she quickly goes. Shutting the door.

A long beat.

Hugo and Isabelle look at each other.

They hear the muffled sounds of Mama Jeanne and Georges
talking in another room.

Whispers:

                    HUGO
          She looked at the armoire.

                    ISABELLE
          I already searched it when I was
          looking for your notebook.

                    HUGO
          I'll look again. You stand guard!

                    ISABELLE
          Splendid!

Hugo opens the armoire and searches through it.

Isabelle, meanwhile, goes to the door.

Peeks through the keyhole.

                                                        (CONTINUED)

Through the keyhole: Georges and Jeanne are across the
apartment, in the kitchen. She is pouring coffee. She steals
a nervous glance to the bedroom door.

Hugo rifles through the armoire. Clothes. Sheets. No clues.
No treasure. Nothing.

Hugo steps back, studies the outside of the tall armoire.

He notices something:

A decorative panel at the very top of the armoire has two
thin parallel cracks in it.

                    HUGO
          Look!

                    ISABELLE
          We have to investigate!

He carries a chair to the armoire.

                    ISABELLE
          Let me, I'm taller.

She climbs up on the chair and examines the decorative panel.
She has to stand on her tiptoes to reach it.

He makes a gesture for her to knock on it.

She does so.

It sounds hollow.

They are both excited.

She carefully grips the edges of the decorative panel. She
pulls. She pulls again. The panel comes off in her hands!
Revealing...

A hidden compartment at the top of the armoire!

A large box is inside the compartment.

Isabelle hands down the panel to Hugo. Then she begins to
pull the box out. But it is heavy. She struggles a bit.

He holds the chair steady.

She almost has the box out now...

                                              (CONTINUED)

But it is ungainly, she was unprepared for the weight, and she is still balancing on her tiptoes...

As she pulls the box out...

She loses her balance...

The chair lurches...

She almost falls...

But miraculously gets her balance...

Shoots a relieved glance down to Hugo...

But...

Then a leg of the chair SNAPS--!

She falls--

Shrieks--

Hugo catches her--

The box falls--

CRASHES to the floor--

SMASHING open--

Sending up a cyclone of paper--

Hundreds of pieces of paper of every shape and size scatter across the floor and fly through the air--

Hugo and Isabelle are surrounded by a tornado of paper, it swirls around them--

On the paper--

Wonderful drawings. Fanciful and imaginative. Dragons and devils. Spaceships and submarines. Fairies and fish. Elaborate landscapes of fantasy...

One of the drawings seems to slow as it whirls past Hugo...

The man in the moon, a rocket protruding from his right eye...

57   CONTINUED: 57

The swirling papers finally descend to earth...

Revealing...

Georges.

Standing in the doorway. Mama Jeanne behind him.

Georges looks at the carpet of drawings spread out before him.

                    GEORGES
                  (whispers)
            Back from the dead ...

His quiet anguish gives way to anger--

He wades into the drawings--

Grabbing handfuls--

Tearing them up--

Shredding them violently--

Flinging them away--

Mama Jeanne grabs him:

                    MAMA JEANNE
            Stop it, Georges! Stop! This is your
            work!

                    GEORGES
            My work?! -- What am I? Nothing but a
            penniless merchant! A broken windup
            toy!

He spins on Hugo in fury:

                    GEORGES
            I trusted you -- and this is how you
            thank me?! You cruel -- cruel--

Suddenly he can't speak--

Something's wrong -- he gulps for air--

Mama Jeanne sits him on the bed. He is exhausted, gasping for breath.

                                              (CONTINUED)

57   CONTINUED: 57

His sad eyes gaze over the chaos of drawings.

He whispers.

> GEORGES
> An empty box, an old rocket, a lost
> monster ... nothing, nothing,
> nothing...

> MAMA JEANNE
> I'm sorry, Georges ... I'm so sorry...

Isabelle takes Hugo's arm and gently pulls him out.

He glances back.

Sees Mama Jeanne tenderly holding her disconsolate husband.

Hugo is haunted by the poignant image.

58   EXT. APARTMENT - EVENING   58

Evening. Street lamps are coming on, illuminate the scene.

Isabelle is at the front door.

A beat.

> ISABELLE
> I should go back.

> HUGO
> Okay.

A beat.

> ISABELLE
> I've never seen him cry before.

Hugo takes her hand.

A comforting gesture of friendship.

She acknowledges it.

A faint smile.

She starts to close the door. Stops.

58   CONTINUED: 58

                              ISABELLE
                    Thank you for the movie today ... It
                    was a gift.

She shuts the door.

Hugo walks down the street.

He stops under the street lamp for a moment. Gazing back up
at the apartment.

59   INT. TRAIN STATION -- GRAND HALL - EVENING   59

Hugo enters. Deep in thought. Head down.

He's not looking and accidentally bumps right into--

The frosty Monsieur Labisse! Labisse drops a few books he was
carrying. Hugo quickly picks them up:

                              HUGO
                    Oh, I'm sorry, sir!

He notices one of the books is the French ROBIN HOOD he was
looking at before. He smiles when he sees it.

                         MONSIEUR LABISSE
                    You know that volume?

                              HUGO
                    I used to read it with my father...

                         MONSIEUR LABISSE
                    Hm ... It was intended for my godson. But now I
                    think it is intended for you.
                         (slight formal bow)
                    Monsieur Cabret.

Labisse goes, leaving Hugo with the book. Hugo is shocked by
his unexpected act of kindness.

Hugo continues on.

He sees the Station Inspector sitting at the outside section
of the cafe, sipping a tiny cup of demitasse. Hugo slips away
in the other direction.

                                                        (CONTINUED)

The station Inspector gazes at the lovely Lisette at her flower stall across the terminal. The object of his affection.

Madame Emilie is watching the Inspector, she knows exactly what's going on.

>   STATION INSPECTOR
>   (re: demitasse)
>   May I have another cup?

>   MADAME EMILIE
>   It's still brewing. Soon...
>   Demitasse, like everything else,
>   must happen at the opportune
>   moment.

The Station Inspector looks at Lisette. Sighs.

>   STATION INSPECTOR
>   If we only knew when that moment
>   was...

>   MADAME EMILIE
>   Be intrepid, my friend. Say hello
>   to her ... Go on. Give me your best
>   smile.

The Station Inspector tries on his best and brightest smile: sort of a pained grimace.

>   MADAME EMILIE
>   Ahh ... Radiant!

The Station Inspector summons up his nerve and heads toward Lisette. He freshens his maladroit smile as he "casually" arrives.

>   STATION INSPECTOR
>   Mademoiselle Lisette, a very gracious
>   good evening to you.

>   LISETTE
>   (shy)
>   Monsieur Inspector.

>   STATION INSPECTOR
>   Hm. Yes ... Those are lovely posies there.

Just then his <u>leg brace seizes up</u>. He tries to remain
nonchalant as he wrestles with unlocking it.

> LISETTE
> They're from Gourdon. They come in
> on the overnight train.

> STATION INSPECTOR
> Ah, Gourdon. Splendid country that.
> Robust! All the ... lovely cows and
> such ... Are they, hm, smelly?

He leans in to sniff the irises. This causes his leg brace to
<u>squeak awkwardly</u>. He stiffens.

She glances to his brace. He sees her glance.

A moment between them.

He nods stiffly. Turns to go.

Walks a few steps.

But then he stops ... No. He will not be ashamed ... He
returns to her.

> STATION INSPECTOR
> You see I was injured in the war. It
> will never heal ... Good evening to
> you, Mademoiselle.

He turns to go. But...

> LISETTE
> I lost my brother.

> STATION INSPECTOR
> Where?

> LISETTE
> Verdun.

His eyes are sympathetic. He was there. He knows.

A beat.

Neither is sure what to do. How to proceed.

Then she smiles shyly, snaps off a blossom, and tucks it into
his lapel.

59   CONTINUED: 59

                            LISETTE
                  Good evening, Monsieur Inspector.

                            STATION INSPECTOR
                       (bows)
                  Good evening, Mademoiselle Lisette.

He goes. His leg brace squeaking proudly.

And we fade to...

A60   INT. TRAIN STATION -- BOOKSTORE - DAY   A60

Monsieur Labisse is at the counter, reading one of his
beloved antique tomes.

Hugo and Isabelle are nearby, busy looking through a stack of
old books.

                            HUGO
                  ... I can't find anything about old
                  movies.

                            ISABELLE
                  How vexatious!

Monsieur Labisse never glances up from his tome:

                            MONSIEUR LABISSE
                  You'll have to go to the Film
                  Academy Library.

                            ISABELLE
                  Excuse me?

                            MONSIEUR LABISSE
                       (still reading)
                  For books about old movies you must
                  go to the Film Academy
                  Library...THE INVENTION OF DREAMS
                  by Rene Tabard...
                       (continues mysteriously)
                  2nd level. Row Four. Section Three.
                  Top Shelf.

                            HUGO
                       (bows)
                  Thank you, Monsieur Labisse.

                                                          (CONTINUED)

A60   CONTINUED: A60

                          MONSIEUR LABISSE
                       (nods)
                    Monsieur Cabret.

Hugo and Isabelle go.

Monsieur Labisse finally looks up. Watches then go. Smiles.

60   OMITTED   60

61   OMITTED   61

62   INT. FILM ACADEMY -- LIBRARY - DAY   62

Hugo and Isabelle, tiny figures, move through a vast,
intimidating and cathedral-quiet library.

Two stories. Shining brass fixtures and rich wooden shelves.
Neats rows of books. Imperial.

They climb some stairs, and move through the stacks to find
Row Four, Section Three. They pull down a large book from the
top shelf.

Above them is a beautiful ceiling mural of Prometheus: a
magical ray of light shooting from his hand.

They go to a library table and look at the book:

THE INVENTION OF DREAMS: THE STORY OF THE FIRST MOVIES by
Rene Tabard.

Hugo runs his hands over the cover.

He glances to Isabelle.

This could be it. The answer to their quest.

He opens the book.

They begin to read:

                                                        (CONTINUED)

                         HUGO (V.O.)
            "In 1895, one of the very first films
            ever shown was called A TRAIN ARRIVES
            IN THE STATION, which showed nothing
            more than a train coming into a
            station..."

We *see the little film* of the train steaming into the
station.

                         ISABELLE (V.O.)
            "But when the train came speeding
            toward the screen, the audience
            screamed because they thought they
            were in danger of being run over. No
            one had ever seen anything like it
            before."

Hugo smiles to her:

                         HUGO
            No one had ever seen anything like it
            before.

They turn the page...

And we go with them...

INTO THE BOOK...

Flickering images from the very first movies...

Fragile fragments of life captured forever...

A stream of factory workers leaving work ... Two Edison
technicians dancing ... Skyscrapers in New York ... London
street scene ... a boxing match ...

                         HUGO (V.O.)
            "What began as a sideshow novelty
            soon grew into something more as the
            first filmmakers discovered they
            could use the new medium to tell
            stories..."

And now we see storytelling and narrative replacing the
quaint real life images...

Edison's THE KISS ... THE GREAT TRAIN ROBBERY ... THE CABINET
OF DR. CALIGARI ... INTOLERANCE ... Buster Keaton ...

(CONTINUED)

62   CONTINUED: 62

Louise Brooks ... William S. Hart ... Doug Fairbanks ... Jean Renoir...

The splendid, magical, romantic, lost world of silent movies flickers past...

Hugo and Isabelle fan the pages of the book back and forth, searching...

And then...

The culmination of the whole sequence...

We end at one iconic image...

Glowing with light...

A TRIP TO THE MOON.

The man in the moon with a rocket protruding from his eye.

Hugo and Isabelle stare at the image.

They share an excited glance.

                    ISABELLE
               (reads)
          "The filmmaker Georges Melies was among
          the first to realized that film had the
          power to capture dreams..."

                    HUGO
               (reads)
          "This great pioneer of early cinema
          died during the Great War--"

                    ISABELLE
          Died...?

                    HUGO
               (reads)
          "Died during the Great War."

They stop. Stunned.

Unbeknownst to them, a tall and imposing figure has been looming over them. Observing.

PROFESSOR RENE TABARD is a formidable presence. Stern and uncompromising.

                                                    (CONTINUED)

62   CONTINUED: 62

                         TABARD
                You're interested in Melies?

The kids jump -- slam the book shut almost guiltily.

                         HUGO
                Yes, uh--

                         ISABELLE
                It's allowed.

                         TABARD
                Is it?

A long, cool, appraising stare.

Then Hugo realizes something -- he nudges Isabelle -- the
photo on the back of the book shows the author:

Rene Tabard. The same man who is standing before them.

                         ISABELLE
                He's my godfather, you see. And very
                much alive thank you very much!

                         TABARD
                But ... that's not possible ...

                         HUGO
                I assure you, sir, it's true.

                         TABARD
                Melies alive...?

Emotion fills his features. A softening. Wonder and joy.

                         TABARD
                Then this day ... is a miracle.

He looks at them. Tears in his eyes.

                         TABARD
                Come with me.

63   INT. FILM ACADEMY -- TABARD'S OFFICE - DAY   63

A door opens into ... the world of Georges Melies.

Professor Tabard's office is something of a shrine to Melies.

                                                    (CONTINUED)

Tattered old movie posters, film stills and handbills for
magic shows line the walls.

Mountains of books, photographs and archival records. Also a
few props and costume pieces lovingly preserved.

Tabard shows Hugo and Isabelle some of the photographs and
artifacts:

                    TABARD
          Here he is at work in his studio
          ... And this is a handbill for his
          stage act ... Here's the great
          Crystal Mystery clock he made.
          Wonderful, isn't it? ... And this
          is one of his actual cameras!

                    ISABELLE
          Why do you have all this?

                    TABARD
          Your godfather is a passion of mine.
          He was a great filmmaker.

                    HUGO
              (looking at a photo)
          He was a magician?

They look at a photo of showing a YOUNG GEORGES on a stage
doing a magic trick:

                    TABARD
          Yes, he began on the stage.

                    ISABELLE
          How did he start making movies?

                    TABARD
          No one really knows.

Hugo has been studying the old photographs and
Daguerreotypes. Something special strikes him about them...

                    HUGO
          Look how happy he is...

Indeed, the joy and passion on Young Georges' face is a
marked difference to the moody old man we know.

Isabelle turns to Tabard with a smile.

                                             (CONTINUED)

63   CONTINUED: 63

                         ISABELLE
               Professor Tabard ... Would you like to
               meet him?

                         TABARD
               Oh, but you see, I have met him.

He smiles. The color fades as we go into Tabard's memory...

As with Hugo's flashback earlier, this has the quality of a
SILENT FILM. The flickering, glowing luminescence of early
movies...

64   EXT. FLASHBACK -- GREENHOUSE STUDIO - DAY   64

In the country, outside Paris.

YOUNG TABARD is with his Brother. Young Tabard, around ten,
is staring at something, awed at what he is seeing.

                         TABARD (V.O.)
               My brother worked as a carpenter
               building sets for Melies. One day he
               took me to visit the studio...

We see what Young Tabard has been gazing at:

George Melies' film studio.

The studio is an absolutely astounding sight. A great
greenhouse-like collection of glass rooms. A soaring castle
of glass:

                         TABARD (V.O.)
               It was like something out of a
               dream. The whole building was made
               of glass ... In reality this was to
               let in all the sunlight necessary
               for filming, but to my eyes it was
               nothing short of an enchanted castle
               ... a palace made of glass...

Young Tabard and his Brother go into the studio...

65   INT. FLASHBACK -- GREENHOUSE STUDIO - DAY   65

YOUNG GEORGES is at the camera. Lining up the shot.

                                                  (CONTINUED)

65   CONTINUED: 65

Young Tabard sits quietly and watches.

Young Georges glances over to Young Tabard. Sees the
enchanted look in the boy's eyes. Smiles.

                    YOUNG GEORGES
          If you've ever wondered where your
          dreams come from, you look around.
          This is where they're made.

66   INT. FILM ACADEMY -- TABARD'S OFFICE - DAY   66

                    TABARD
          In the end, he made over 500 movies
          ... He was phenomenally popular in
          his day.

                    ISABELLE
          But why did he stop?

                    TABARD
          Up until today, I believed that he
          died in the war, like so many
          others.

                    HUGO
          Can we watch some of his movies?

                    TABARD
          I wish you could ... But time hasn't
          been kind to old movies...

He goes to his desk. Unlocks a drawer. Reverently removes a
cannister of film.

                    TABARD
          This is the only one that we know of
          that survived ... Out of hundreds
          ... One.

Tabard is moved, looking at the single sad cannister of film.

He looks up at them.

                    TABARD
          And still ... it is a masterpiece.

67   INT. TRAIN STATION -- HANGING CLOCK - AFTERNOON   67

Isabelle is accompanying Hugo on his rounds as he winds the clocks.

They climb down the long ladder into the large clock suspended from the ceiling of the Grand Hall. He has his bucket of tools.

Clock dials surround him on all four sides.

                    HUGO
    ... I think it's the only way.
    He'll be excited. Why wouldn't he
    be?

He checks his pocket watch, then uses a little screwdriver to tinker with one of the clocks.

Isabelle stays above on the ladder, pokes her head down:

                    ISABELLE
    Do you think I should tell Mama Jeanne?

                    HUGO
    No, it has to be a surprise, like a
    magic trick. We have to have some
    ... panache.

                    ISABELLE
      (impressed with the word)
    Well done.

Just then--

Through one of the clock faces--

Hugo sees the Station Inspector and Maximilian!

Approaching. Stopping.

Standing directly below the clock!

Hugo urgently gestures up to her to be quiet:

                    HUGO
    Shhh!

He points down.

                                    (CONTINUED)

CONTINUED:

She sees the Station Inspector.

A long beat.

Hugo doesn't dare breathe.

The Station Inspector stands there, comparing the time on his various watches to the time of the suspended clock. Then he starts to go.

Hugo exhales. Safe.

But...

Then...

Hugo's foot hits his tool bag, knocking a little spanner away...

It falls...

Hugo grabs for it...

Isabelle watches in horror...

Hugo misses...

The spanner falls...

It hits the station floor with a resounding...

CLINK!

The Station Inspector and Maximilian both stop. Instantly turning their heads, ears alert, like identical dogs.

                    STATION INSPECTOR
          Monsieur Claude? Are you up there?
          ... Monsieur Claude?

Hugo looks up to Isabelle in panic.

What should he do?!

Unruffled, she signals him to stay calm.

The Station Inspector goes. Maximilian gives a nasty glance back, but follows.

Hugo looks up at Isabelle.

67   CONTINUED: 67

That was close!

68   INT. TRAIN STATION -- LOBBY CLOCK - AFTERNOON   68

Hugo kneels to wind the clock, which is at foot level.
Isabelle sits next to him.

                    HUGO
          ... It's the only way we'll find out
          everything ... Papa Georges will see
          that there are people who remember
          him. How can that be wrong?

                    ISABELLE
               (hesitant)
          I don't know...

                    HUGO
          Please, Isabelle ... My father, the
          Automaton, Papa Georges, it's like a
          puzzle ... When we put it all
          together, something's going to
          happen.

                    ISABELLE
          A message from your father?

He doesn't look at her.

                    HUGO
          Maybe.

                    ISABELLE
          I just hope ... you won't be disappointed.

A beat as he works on the clock.

Through the face of the clock Hugo sees Monsieur Labisse at
the door of his shop, taking delivery of some books.

                    HUGO
          Monsieur Labisse gave me a book
          last night.

                    ISABELLE
          He's always doing that. Sending
          books to a good home, that's what
          he calls it.

                                              (CONTINUED)

> HUGO
> He's got a real ... <u>purpose</u>.

> ISABELLE
> What do you mean?

> HUGO
> (points)
> Could you hand me that?

She hands him a tool from the bucket.

She flops over on her back, looking up at him as he continues to work on the clock:

> HUGO
> I mean ... Did you ever notice that
> all machines are made for some
> <u>reason</u>? They make you laugh, like
> Papa Georges' toys, or they tell
> time, like the clocks ... Maybe
> that's why broken machines always
> make me sad, because they can't do
> what they're meant to do.

She looks up at him. From her perspective, he is beautifully framed by the intricate clockwork.

> HUGO
> Maybe it's the same with people.
> If you lose your purpose ... it's
> like you're broken.

> ISABELLE
> Like Papa Georges.

> HUGO
> Maybe we can fix him.

He continues to work on the clock.

A beat as she watches him.

> ISABELLE
> Is that your purpose?

> HUGO
> What?

68   CONTINUED: 68

> ISABELLE
> That. Fixing things.

> HUGO
> I don't know. It's what my father did.

> ISABELLE
> I wonder what my purpose is?

> HUGO
> I don't know.

A long beat as she thinks about it.

It seems to make her sad.

> ISABELLE
> Maybe if I had known my parents I would know.

She gazes out over the terminal, a little lost.

He looks at her. Senses her sadness.

A beat.

> HUGO
> Come with me.

69   INT. TRAIN STATION -- CLOCK TOWER - EVENING   69

The enormous clock.

The majestic view of Paris.

The lights of the city are twinkling on. It is magical. The whole city seems to move and flow like an elegant, perfect machine.

Hugo and Isabelle look over the city.

> HUGO
> Right after my father died, I
> would come up here a lot ... I
> would imagine that the whole world
> was one big machine. Machines
> never have any extra parts, you
> know. They always have the exact
> number they need.

69   CONTINUED: 69

                    So I figured if the entire world
                    was a big machine I couldn't be an
                    extra part, I had to be here for
                    some reason ... And that means you
                    have to be here for some reason,
                    too.

She is touched.

Paris sparkles below. Like it is made of stars.

The only sound is the steady, rhythmic pulse of the clock's
machinery.

She gently takes his hand.

A huge full moon is rising.

They are silhouetted before the glowing moon.

And above them the solar system is spinning away in perfect
order. The spheres in harmony. Like a great clockwork
mechanism.

70   INT. TRAIN STATION -- TOY BOOTH - EVENING   70

Georges is closing up the shop. His movement are slow and
leaden.

Hugo and Isabelle are hiding around a corner:

                    HUGO
             I'll bring them at seven o'clock
             tomorrow night. Don't say anything.

                    ISABELLE
             Are you sure about this?

                    HUGO
             Not really ... But I think it's the
             only way...

                    ISABELLE
             To fix him.

He nods.

A beat.

She impulsively gives him a quick kiss on the cheek.

                                                        (CONTINUED)

70   CONTINUED: 70

He is shocked.

Then she runs to Georges at the Toy Booth.

Hugo slips away.

71   INT. TRAIN STATION -- TUNNELS - EVENING   71

Hugo watches from behind a clock face.

He sees Georges and Isabelle leaving the station.

72   INT. TRAIN STATION -- SECRET APARTMENT - NIGHT   72

Candles are burning.

Hugo is getting ready for bed. Carefully winding his big
pocket watch. Hanging it on its special hook by the bed.

He looks at the Automaton.

The Automaton looks back at him.

Hugo blows out the candles and settles into bed.

He is nervous about tomorrow.

We hear the steady tick ... tick ... tick ... of his
pocket watch. The rhythmic sounds is conforting.

Hugo finally shuts his eyes. Sleeps.

The Automaton watches him. Concerned.

72A   INT. TRAIN STATION -- PLATFORM - MORNING   72A

Lovely morning. Hugo has slept well.

He's moving along one of the platforms, scouting for
breakfast opportunities, when he notices something on the
train tracks.

Shining. Catching his eye.

... It looks like Isabelle's heart-shaped key. He's confused.
He can't see it clearly.

72A   CONTINUED: 72A

A quick look around and he jumps down onto the tracks. He
roots around in the soot. Picks it up. <u>It is Isabelle's key.</u>
Or one very much like it. He turns it over. Engraved on the
back: "Cabret and Son. Horologists."

What does this mean? He's so engrossed in this strange new
mystery that he doesn't see...

<u>A train is speeding into the station</u>!

Right at him--

Finally he feels the vibration--

He spins--

THE TRAIN IS RIGHT ON TOP OF HIM--!

Screeching train whistle, screaming brakes--

Hugo tries to leap away--

Too late--

A great rush of steam as the train barrels in--

Way too fast -- out of control -- can't stop -- screams --
panic --

<u>AS THE TRAIN CRASHES THROUGH THE STATION</u>!!

It leaps the tracks and smashes through the barriers -- rips
across the Grand Hall -- shredding marble and glass and metal
-- people dive out of the way --

The runaway train continues its rampage -- crashing through
the cafe -- shattering the flower stall -- tearing into the
lobby and finally--

SMASHING through the facade of the building itself--!

CAREENING outside -- CRASHING to the street below -- the
locomotive engine tilting precariously--!

Then--!

72B   INT. TRAIN STATION -- SECRET APARTMENT - DAY   72B

--Hugo bolts awake!

(CONTINUED)

72B   CONTINUED: 72B

It's all been a nightmare.

He sits there. Trying to catch his breath.

We hear the steady tick ... tick ... tick of Hugo's pocket
watch.

But something is wrong.

Tick ... tick ... tick ... it sounds <u>different</u> now...

He glances over. The pocket watch isn't hanging from its hook
anymore.

He listens intently...

Tick ... tick ... tick ...

The sound appears to be coming from...

From him!

He pulls his shirt aside to reveal--

His guts are a ticking, spinning clockwork--

He bolts up--

He is a machine!

An Automaton!

And the apartment around him is now an ENORMOUS MACHINE. Loud
and horrible. He is utterly surrounded. POUNDING pistons.
GRINDING gears. SPINNING wheels.

The Hugo's face--

Starts to melt away--

Beginning to be replaced by the impassive features of the
Automaton--

Then--

73   OMITTED   73

STILLS

Asa Butterfield plays Hugo Cabret.

All photos by Jaap Buitendijk
© 2011 GK Films, LLC.
All Rights Reserved.

Sacha Baron Cohen plays the Station Inspector.

Hugo runs through a café, chased by the Station Inspector and his guard dog.

Hugo cleverly avoids the Station Inspector again.

Emily Mortimer plays Lisette.

Hugo works on the automaton with his father, played by Jude Law.

Hugo tries to learn a card trick from Georges Méliès, played by Ben Kingsley.

Isabelle, played by Chloë Grace Moretz, and Hugo sneak into the train station, watched by the Station Inspector.

Director Martin Scorsese shows Asa Butterfield and Chloë Grace Moretz an illustration from Brian Selznick's book.

Left to right: Chloë Grace Moretz and Asa Butterfield discuss a scene with director Martin Scorsese.

Hugo takes Isabelle on an adventure to the cinema.

Hugo is astonished to find that Isabelle has the mysterious heart-shaped key on a chain around her neck.

Hugo and Isabelle are amazed to watch the automaton write on his own.

The bookstore owner, Monsieur Labisse, played by Christopher Lee, gives Hugo a copy of *Robin Hood*.

Isabelle discovers how Hugo keeps the station clock working properly.

Hugo Cabret watches from the vantage point of the clock.

Ben Kingsley plays Georges Méliès.

Rene Tabard, played by Michael Stuhlbarg, excitedly shows his Méliès collection to Isabelle and Hugo.

The Station Inspector catches Hugo, who clutches his automaton.

Hugo and Isabelle proudly applaud at the ceremony for Georges Méliès at
the Film Academy theatre.

Ben Kingsley (center right, as Georges Méliès) confers with director/producer Martin Scorsese (far right) on the set.

Director/Producer Martin Scorsese (center) on the set.

74   INT. TRAIN STATION -- SECRET APARTMENT - NIGHT   74

--Hugo jerks awake.

Panting for air.

He gets out of bed. Lights a candle.

Sits.

He won't sleep anymore tonight.

He glances to the Automaton. It looks back at him. Worried.

75   OMITTED   75

75A   EXT. BANKS OF THE SEINE - MORNING   75A

The soles of two big shoes. Facing us.

They're attached to a body covered by a sheet. Two GENDARMES
standing over it.

One of them pulls a flask from the body. Looks at it.

Engraved on the flask: *"Claude Cabret."*

Ringing phone takes us to--

75B   INT. TRAIN STATION -- INSPECTOR'S OFFICE - DAY   75B

The Station Inspector is on the phone:

                    STATION INSPECTOR
          ... Yes, he's employed here ...
          Deceased?! ... But then who has
          been winding the clocks?!

76   EXT. APARTMENT BUILDING - NIGHT   76

Hugo waits nervously outside Georges' building. He checks his
big pocket watch. It is just after 7:00.

Professor Tabard approaches through the graveyard across the
street. He carries something in a large wooden box.

                                                        (CONTINUED)

76   CONTINUED: 76

                              TABARD
                    Good evening.

                              HUGO
                    This way, sir.

He leads Tabard into the building.

77   INT. APARTMENT - NIGHT   77

Isabelle is pretending to read.

Mama Jeanne is across the room, sewing. Georges is nowhere to
be seen.

There is a knock at the door.

Isabelle gives a little yelp and jumps up:

                              ISABELLE
                    I'll get it!

Jeanne removes her heavy glasses, curious, as Isabelle
hurries to the door and opens it.

                              ISABELLE
                    Oh, what a surprise! Come in, come in...

Hugo and Tabard enter.

                              MAMA JEANNE
                    What is the meaning of this, Isabelle?

                              ISABELLE
                    Please don't be mad.

                              MAMA JEANNE
                    That young man is not welcome here.

                              HUGO
                    We found out who Papa Georges is.

A beat as she stares at them.

The imposing Rene Tabard steps forward, polite and formal.

                              TABARD
                    I deeply apologize, Madame. I
                    thought you were expecting us.

                                                        (CONTINUED)

> I will leave immediately and return
> upon your request.

MAMA JEANNE
> Please, keep your voices down, my
> husband is sleeping. He hasn't been
> well ... I ... I'm afraid you will
> not be invited back.

ISABELLE
> Don't make them leave...

TABARD
> I don't want to impose on you, Madame
> Melies, but if this is to be the only
> time we meet, please let me express
> to you the profound debt of gratitude
> I owe your husband.

She looks at him.

TABARD
> When I was boy I saw all his films.
> They inspired me ... Your husband is a
> very great artist.

She is touched.

MAMA JEANNE
> I'm pleased that you remember my
> husband's films with such
> fondness, but he's become so
> fragile ... It only hurts him to
> remember the past.

TABARD
> (bows)
> Then we will take our leave, Madame
> ... And I do hope you'll forgive me
> for saying, you are as lovely now
> as you were in the movies.

Hugo and Isabelle are stunned.

ISABELLE
> Mama Jeanne...?

HUGO
> You were in the movies?

(CONTINUED)

                           TABARD
               She appeared in almost all of his films.

                           ISABELLE
               You were an actress?!

                           MAMA JEANNE
               That was a long time ago, children.
               Another life ... I was another
               person.

                           TABARD
               Would you like to meet her again?

Mama Jeanne looks at him, curious.

                           TABARD
               We have a film.

                           MAMA JEANNE
               One of Georges' films...? But that's
               not possible. They're all gone.

                           TABARD
               May we show you?

Hugo and Isabelle implore Mama Jeanne:

                           HUGO
               Oh, please...

                           ISABELLE
               Please, Mama Jeanne...

Mama Jeanne glances quickly to the closed bedroom door.

                           MAMA JEANNE
               Be quick with it.

Rene Tabard opens the wooden box. It contains a portable
movie projector. He sets it up, plugs it in, and threads a
film, as:

                           ISABELLE
               An actress! A cinema actress! It's
               impossibly romantic!

                           MAMA JEANNE
               It wasn't like that. We weren't
               movie stars like they have now ...

                                                    (CONTINUED)

CONTINUED:

> (a certain twinkle in her eye)
> But we did have fun.

Tabard has finished. The projector is ready to go. Facing a blank wall.

                    TABARD
          Madame Melies?

She nods.

Tabard turns on the projector.

Flickering white light.

A TRIP TO THE MOON.

We see selections from the fantastical Georges Melies film, giving us a sense of this delightful movie.

For Mama Jeanne the emotion is overwhelming. Like seeing the past come to life. Her eyes fill with tears.

The wizard-like Astronomers argue in the great hall.

The rocket is constructed in a busy workshop. The huge cannon is tested. Then it is time for the rocket to be launched.

Pretty girls line up and usher the five voyagers into the rocket.

During this sequence one particular girl is featured.

She is in the foreground. Lovely.

                    ISABELLE
          Mama Jeanne ... it's you!

                    MAMA JEANNE
          Yes...

The great cannon is fired.

Then the famous sequence. We zoom toward the moon. The face of the man in the moon appears. The rocket hits him in the right eye! He reacts.

Once we reach the moon, the movie is in <u>color</u>. Lovely and diffused. Pale pastels.

                        HUGO
            It's color!

                        MAMA JEANNE
            We tinted the film ... Painted it by hand.

*The voyagers move around the lunar surface. The earth rises
over the horizon. Fantasy images of comets shooting past,
stars, planets, constellations. Then it snows and the
voyagers go into a crater.*

*Inside the moon, a weird landscape. Bizarre Moon Creatures
appear. The voyagers battle them. The Moon Creatures
disappear magically in puffs of smoke.*

*The voyagers escape into the rocket. It is pulled off the
edge of the moon.*

*The rocket soars back to earth. It splashes into the ocean
and goes underwater. An enchanting bottom-of-the-sea setting.*

The rocket is finally towed back to shore.

The movie ends.

The film tail flips around.

The white light flickers.

A beat.

Mama Jeanne is drying her eyes.

Isabelle takes her hand.

                        ISABELLE
            You were so beautiful.

A voice, from behind them:

                        GEORGES (O.S.)
            She still is.

They turn.

Georges is standing in the doorway. He has seen it all.

                        GEORGES
            I would recognize the sound of a
            movie projector anywhere.

77   CONTINUED: 77

Mama Jeanne goes to him and holds him closely.

She helps him to sit.

He is emotionally drained.

She looks at Georges deeply.

                    MAMA JEANNE
          Georges ... You've tried to forget
          the past for so long, and that's
          brought you nothing but unhappiness
          ... Maybe it's time to remember.

She takes his hands in hers.

                    MAMA JEANNE
          I remember the man I fell in love with
          ... I don't want to lose him forever.

A long moment between them.

Georges kisses her hands.

He turns, studies Hugo.

                    GEORGES
          You want to know?

                    HUGO
          Yes.

A beat.

So be it.

                    GEORGES
          Like you ... I loved to fix things...

The color drains from the scene as Georges remembers...

78   INT. FLASHBACK -- MAGIC THEATRE - NIGHT   78

Like the flashbacks earlier, Georges' story has the quality
of a *SILENT FILM*.

Flickering gaslight. We see YOUNG GEORGES on stage. YOUNG
JEANNE is his assistant. They do a magic trick.

78   CONTINUED: 78

                        GEORGES (V.O.)
              I started out as a magician, and
              Mama Jeanne was my assistant. We
              were very successful, I must say.
              We even had our own theatre...

79   INT. FLASHBACK -- THEATRE/BACKSTAGE - NIGHT   79

Young Georges is tinkering with something mechanical we don't
see.

                        GEORGES (V.O.)
              But I was always tinkering with
              machines. I had my own workshop at the
              theatre where I could invent new
              illusions ... Once I even built a
              working Automaton. Ah, he was a
              particular treasure. I put my heart
              and soul into him...

We see that Young Georges has been working on the
Automaton...

80   EXT. FLASHBACK -- CIRCUS GROUNDS - NIGHT   80

Young Georges and Young Jeanne enjoy a night at a traveling
circus. They move past sideshow tents.

                        GEORGES (V.O.)
              Then one night, Mama Jeanne and I
              went to visit a traveling circus.
              We were walking past the sideshow
              tents when I noticed something ...
              Something strange ... Something
              wonderful...

In the distance, Young Georges sees bright light flickering
magically from one of the sideshow tents. The light draws him
like a moth to a flame...

81   INT. FLASHBACK -- SIDESHOW TENT - NIGHT   81

Young Georges and Young Jeanne are in the sideshow tent.
Watching a very early movie. Both are transported.

                                                        (CONTINUED)

81   CONTINUED: 81

> GEORGES (V.O.)
> The Lumiere brothers had invented the
> movies. I fell in love with their
> invention. How could I not be a part
> of it? It was like a new kind of
> magic...

82   INT. FLASHBACK -- THEATRE/BACKSTAGE - DAY   82

Young Georges uses spare pieces from the Automaton to make a
movie camera. It is a beautiful and elaborate creation.

> GEORGES (V.O.)
> I asked the Lumiere brothers to
> sell me a camera, but they refused.
> You see they were convinced the
> movies were only a passing fad and
> saw no future in it. Or so they
> said ... But like Edison in America
> and R.W. Paul in England, I just
> had to be a part of this new
> wonder. We were like explorers
> then, getting lost, finding our way
> ... In the end I built my own
> camera using leftover pieces from
> the Automaton...

83   EXT. FLASHBACK -- GREENHOUSE STUDIO - DAY   83

In the country, outside Paris. Young Georges and Young Jeanne
pose proudly in front of their new studio as a photographer
exposes a picture.

> GEORGES (V.O.)
> We risked everything ... We sold
> the theatre and everything we had
> so we could build our own movie
> studio...

84   INT. FLASHBACK -- GREENHOUSE STUDIO - DAY   84

> GEORGES (V.O.)
> And so the great adventure began!
> I wrote, designed, directed and
> acted in hundreds of movies.

84   CONTINUED: 84

> Magic tricks and illusion became
> my specialty; the world of
> imagination ...

... YOUNG GEORGES zealously sketches a beautiful woman
outfitted in an elegant striped costume and silken wings...

84a   ... YOUNG JEANNE wears the same elegant striped costume   84a
amidst a flurry of activity as the crew prepares for shooting
THE DAMNATION OF FAUST. A hairdresser prepares a wig for
Jeanne as a seamstress sews on the silk wings...

84b   ... Georges uses a four foot long paint brush to put the   84b
finishing touches on a monochromatic stage flat that lies on
the floor as other crew members use ropes, pulleys, hammers
and nails to assemble the set...

84c   ... a metronome counts out the rhythm as a cameraman   84c
cranks the camera. In perfect synch, Georges, dressed as
Mephistopheles, strikes a dramatic pose on stage before
disappearing in a cloud of smoke. Stagehands man the trap
door by turning a crank drum.

84d   ... Jeanne shares a laugh with Georges, wiping powder off 84d
of his face...

84e   ... A blast of flame and smoke reveal a great mechanical   84e
dragon, writhing and attacking, jaws snapping, articulated by
puppeteers. Technicians and puppeteers wrestle with the wire-
operated giant as Georges conducts a rehearsal of Arabian
Knights attacking the dragon...

84f   ... in perfect synch with the metronome, an Arabian   84f
knight strikes a running skeleton with his sword. As the
cameraman continues cranking, the actors freeze. Georges
rushes onto set, quickly clearing the fallen skeleton,
directing the special effects men -

> GEORGES (CONT'D)
> Alright everyone, action on the
> count of three. And
> ONE...TWO...THREE!

The technicians set off a puff of smoke where the skeleton
had been and the actors "unfreeze" and continue to act.

84g   Georges sits at an editing table holding the negative. He 84g
cuts the film with a pair of scissors and splices the two
strips together. He then holds the pasted strip up to the
light again and smiles.

84   CONTINUED: 84

84h   The negative splice shows the 2 frames - "before and   84h
          after" - of the trick shot. The negative turns into positive
          film. We see the fruit of Georges' labor as we see the
          sequence play out - the Arabian Knight stabs the skeleton and
          it seamlessly disappears into a cloud of smoke...

84i   We end with a singularly beautiful image: 84i

          Georges places Young Jeanne, dressed as an angelic star-
          angel, onto a black platform fixed with a comet halo (as in a
          photo)...

          Young Jeanne posing as a comet (to match the photo).

                         GEORGES
                   My beautiful wife was my muse, my
                   star, and we couldn't have been
                   happier ... We thought it would
                   never end. How could it?

          Technicians set off an arc of sparklers around Young Jeanne.

          Georges face lights up.

          A blazing rocket shoots past Young Jeanne -- superimposed
          like a lovely shooting star--

          Suddenly--

84j   More pyrotechnics -- but different now -- the EXPLOSION   84j
          OF BOMBS -- flashes of light -- trenches and barbed wire --
          the horrible rattle of machine guns -- iconic images of the
          First World War--

85   EXT. FLASHBACK -- POSTER WALL - DAY   85

          Rain. Gorgeous MOVIE POSTERS being soaked, washing away,
          dissolving...

                         GEORGES (V.O.)
                   But then the war came, and youth and
                   hope were at an end ... The world
                   had no time for magic tricks and
                   movie shows...

          The sodden posters dissolve, taking us to...

86   OMITTED   86

87   EXT. FLASHBACK -- GREENHOUSE STUDIO - NIGHT   87

Georges stands outside the ruins of his studio.

A great bonfire is roaring. We see a huge painted version of
the famous moon face from A TRIP TO THE MOON burning.

Georges, in anguish, is tossing costumes into the pyre.

                    GEORGES (V.O.)
              One night, in bitter despair, I
              burned all my old sets and costumes
              ... I was forced to sell my movies
              to a company that melted them down
              into chemicals used to make shoe
              heels...

A sudden flare from the bonfire--

Transforms to--

A reel of old movie film -- bursting into flames, blazing --
then melting--

The liquid is poured into a mold -- a shoe heel emerges from
the mold -- it is nailed onto a shoe--

The shoe walks past the Toy Booth in the Train Station...

88   INT/EXT. FLASHBACK -- GREENHOUSE STUDIO - DAY/NIGHT   88

TIME LAPSE ... the beautiful greenhouse studio decays ... the
windows crack and break ... weeds spring up ... the gorgeous
set pieces rot ... the roof falls ... rain splashes in ...
the studio is boarded up and abandoned ...

                    GEORGES (V.O.)
              Eventually I couldn't pay the
              actors or keep the business running
              ... And so my enchanted castle fell
              to ruin ... Everything was lost...

89   INT. FLASHBACK - TRAIN STATION -- TOY BOOTH - DAY   89

Georges is in the Toy Booth. It looks much the same, only
newer. It is like a prison.

                                              (CONTINUED)

89   CONTINUED: 89

                         GEORGES (V.O.)
                 With the little money I made from
                 selling my films I bought the toy
                 booth ... And there I have remained...

Georges sits at the counter.

He stares out. Lost. Dead-eyed.

The color gradually returns...

And Georges' face ages to now...

As we return to...

90   INT. APARTMENT - NIGHT   90

... Georges's face.

He concludes the story:

                         GEORGES
                 The only thing I couldn't bring
                 myself to destroy was my beloved
                 Automaton. I gave him to a museum,
                 hoping he would find a home. But they
                 never put him on display. And then
                 the museum burned ... It's all gone
                 now. Everything I ever made ...
                 Nothing but ashes and fading strips
                 of celluloid.

He looks at Hugo deeply.

Proceeds with difficulty:

                         GEORGES
                 My life has taught me one lesson,
                 Hugo ... Not the one I thought it
                 would ... Happy endings only happen
                 in the movies.

                         HUGO
                 The story's not over yet.

He stands. Excited.

                         HUGO
                 I'll be right back!

                                                    (CONTINUED)

90   CONTINUED: 90

He shares a secret look with Isabelle and then runs out.

Georges is mystified.

91   EXT. STREETS - NIGHT   91

Hugo races through the streets.

92   INT. TRAIN STATION -- GRAND HALL - NIGHT   92

Meanwhile, the train station is bustling.

Monsieur Frick is walking through the Grand Hall. He carries
a large picnic basket and has a rather crafty expression.

He approaches Madame Emilie's cafe.

Madame Emilie is pleased to see him. Her dachshund is not. It
begins to growl menacingly.

This time, however, Monsieur Frick is not deterred.

He approaches bravely.

The dachshund growls more. About to attack.

Then...

Monsieur Frick reaches into the picnic basket...

And removes...

Another little dachshund.

With a pink ribbon around its neck.

Madame Emilie's dachshund is instantly smitten. The two dogs
nuzzle affectionately.

Monsieur Frick, the conquering hero, steps forward boldly,
takes Madame Emilie's hand and kisses it.

                    MADAME EMILIE
              Sir, I am undone!

Just then, Hugo appears.

                                                        (CONTINUED)

He is moving quickly toward one of the air vents past the cafe.

But he ducks to the side when the Station Inspector and Maximilian approach the cafe.

Hugo, hidden nearby, overhears:

> STATION INSPECTOR
> There has been ... a disquieting development.

> MONSIEUR FRICK
> What is it?

> STATION INSPECTOR
> The man who winds the clocks,
> Monsieur Claude, has been found --
> <u>deceased</u>.

Hugo stiffens, listens intently.

> STATION INSPECTOR
> They found his body in the Seine. He's
> been down there for months it seems.
> Amongst the fishes. And such.

> MADAME EMILIE
> Oh dear...

Meanwhile, the two dachshunds are sniffing around.

They wander over to where Hugo is hiding. He tries desperately to shoo them away.

Maximilian notices the dachshunds. He pulls at his leash to investigate. The Station Inspector restrains him.

> STATION INSPECTOR
> I can't say I'm surprised this was his
> mortal culmination. He was an
> inebriant of the highest order. Time
> and again I had to warn him about it
> ... These are the wages of sin!

Just then -- the dachshunds begin BARKING like crazy at Hugo--

Maximilian pulls free--

The Station Inspector sees Hugo--!

Hugo bolts, but not fast enough--

Maximilian bounds -- leaps in front of him -- snarling ferociously--

Hugo freezes, terrified--

The Station Inspector grabs him. Captured!

Hugo struggles to free himself.

                    STATION INSPECTOR
          Got you at last!

                    HUGO
          Let me go!

                    MADAME EMILIE
          Don't hurt him!

                    STATION INSPECTOR
          Believe me, he's indestructible.

                    HUGO
          No, you don't understand...
                    (implores Emilie and
                     Frick)
          Help me, please!

                    MONSIEUR FRICK
          We ought to hear him out.

                    STATION INSPECTOR
          Enough! He's been the bane of my
          existence for weeks. Well, no more,
          little monkey.

                    MADAME EMILIE
          You ought to be ashamed! He's only
          a child.

                    STATION INSPECTOR
          This one may be many things, but a
          child he's not!

The Station Inspector drags Hugo away.

Madame Emilie and Monsieur Frick watch, concerned.

93   INT. TRAIN STATION -- INSPECTOR'S OFFICE - NIGHT   93

The Station Inspector drags Hugo into his office...

                    HUGO
          You don't understand -- I have to go!

               STATION INSPECTOR
          You'll go nowhere until your parents
          can be found.

He flings Hugo into a dreadful little cell and slams the door
shut with a resounding clang. Hugo clings to the bars.

                    HUGO
          I don't have any parents!

               STATION INSPECTOR
          Then it's straight to the orphanage with
          you.

The Station Inspector compulsively re-orders and aligns the
things on his desk, his rage building:

               STATION INSPECTOR
          You'll learn a thing or two there, take
          it from me. How to follow orders. How to
          keep to yourself. How to survive without
          a family. Because you don't need them!
          YOU DON'T NEED A FAMILY!

The Station Inspector's fury echoes around the office. He
turns away to his phone...

Hugo quickly pulls out the lock-picking tool he used
before...

The Stations Inspector picks up the phone, taps the cradle
for a connection...

               STATION INSPECTOR
          Yes, hello? hello? ... Connect me with
          the Police headquarters, Seventh
          Arrondissement. Quickly. I need to
          arrange a...

He glances back to Hugo--

The cell door is open! Hugo is gone!

                                              (CONTINUED)

93   CONTINUED: 93

The Station Inspector instantly dives to the fire pole--

<u>Slides down through the trap door--</u>

94   INT. TRAIN STATION -- GRAND HALL - NIGHT   94

Hugo clatters down the stairs outside the Station Inspector's office--

As the Station Inspector appears from beneath his office, dramatically sliding down the fire pole as he bellows--

                      STATION INSPECTOR
            MAXIMILIAN!

Hugo reaches the floor of the terminal--

Maximilian bolts after Hugo --

Hugo weaves wildly through the terminal.

But the Station Inspector is gaining, spidering quickly after him, his leg brace squeaking.

Hugo cuts a path through a crowd of commuters--

The Station Inspector and Maximilian near--

Hugo disappears around a corner--

95   INT. TRAIN STATION -- CORRIDOR -- NIGHT   95

The Station Inspector and Maximilian round the corner after Hugo--

But Hugo has disappeared!

Then the Station Inspector notices an air vent in the wall is slightly ajar.

96   OMITTED   96

97   INT. TRAIN STATION -- TUNNELS - NIGHT   97

Hugo moves through the tunnels.

                                                       (CONTINUED)

97 CONTINUED: 97

Then he hears a sound echoing ominously ... a low growl ...
Maximilian ... No idea where it's coming from...

Hugo stops. Looks.

The growl is closer now! But from where?!

Hugo looks around in desperation. Tunnels in every direction.

Hugo is by the long stairway leading up to the tower. He
decides to escape that way. He disappears up the stairway.

Just as the Station Inspector and Maximilian round a corner.

They stop. Look in various directions. Which way did he go?

Maximilian sniffs. He indicates the steps up.

98 INT. TRAIN STATION -- TOWER STAIRS - NIGHT   98

Hugo's feet pound. His legs pump. He pants for air.

Climbing, climbing, climbing.

The long stairway seems to stretch out wildly below. Like
VERTIGO.

The Station Inspector and Maximilian pursue. Churning up the
long stairway below Hugo.

99 INT./EXT. TRAIN STATION -- CLOCK TOWER - NIGHT   99

Hugo emerges at the very top of the station.

He looks around in panic.

He hears the Station Inspector and Maximilian coming up the
stairs. Huffing and puffing. Feet pounding. Nails clicking.
Leg brace squeaking. Closer and closer.

Hugo's trapped.

Or is he?

He takes a deep breath.

Then...

He climbs <u>through</u> the enormous clock face.

Until he is clinging to the <u>outside</u> of the clock!

A deadly drop below.

Just like Harold Lloyd in SAFETY LAST.

Inside, the Station Inspector and Maximilian appear.

The Station Inspector Looks around. Puzzled.

Maximilian sniffs. Confused.

Then, outside...

The enormous hour hand that Hugo is clinging to...

Lurches...

Almost breaks...

Hugo clings to it desperately, echoing the iconic image from SAFETY LAST.

The abyss below is terrifying.

Hugo doesn't dare cry out.

Inside, the Station Inspector grunts.

                    STATION INSPECTOR
            Must have gone the other way. Come!

He leads Maximilian back down the stairs.

Outside, Hugo carefully pulls himself to safety. He sits on a ledge for a moment. Getting his breath.

He looks over Paris.

Shakes his head.

What a night!

He climbs back through the clock.

100   OMITTED   100

101   INT. TRAIN STATION -- PLATFORM - NIGHT   101

Hugo moves along a platform.

A train has just arrived.

Scores of commuters are climbing off the train and scurrying along the platform.

They jostle Hugo.

He continues on.

Then...

Behind him...

We see...

A bottle-green coat.

The Station Inspector.

Following.

Oddly, no sign of Maximilian.

Hugo shifts the heavy Automaton, trying to make it easier to carry as he pushes through the crowd.

The Station Inspector nears...

Hugo doesn't see him...

The Station Inspector reaches out for Hugo...

But then Hugo sees the Station Inspector's image, reflected in a window of the train.

Hugo cleverly nips BETWEEN TWO TRAIN CARS--

102   OMITTED   102

103   INT. TRAIN STATION -- PLATFORM - NIGHT   103

He emerges to the other side of the platform--

CONTINUED:

Where--

Maximilian is waiting!

Hugo lurches to a stop--

The Station Inspector, who has followed, lunges for Hugo, grabbing his arm--

Swinging him around--

Hugo loses his grip--

The Automaton flies from Hugo's arms!

Time slows as...

The beautiful machine falls through the air...

Tumbling end-over-end...

Falling slowly toward the empty train tracks of the next platform over...

Finally...

Crashing down!

And there's a train coming <u>along these tracks</u>--

Barreling out of the station--

Picking up speed--

Hugo doesn't hesitate--

He jerks his arm free--

Jumps down--

<u>Onto the tracks</u>!

The train is nearing. Coming straight at Hugo. Just like the early movie we saw before, A TRAIN ARRIVES IN THE STATION.

The train gets bigger and bigger as it approaches.

Hugo grabs the Automaton.

The train's whistle howls. Someone screams.

(CONTINUED)

103   CONTINUED: 103

A hand reaches down for Hugo.

The train. Closer and closer.

The metallic screech of the train's brakes.

Hugo thrusts his hand up.

The Station Inspector clasps his hand.

At the last possible moment, Hugo is yanked off the tracks to
safety. He still clings to the Automaton.

A shower of sparks from the train's wheels as it passes.

Hugo and the Automaton fall awkwardly to the platform.

The Station Inspector and the crowd are stunned. They press
in. Questioning. Scolding. Poking. Talking.

Hugo only cares about the Automaton. It is broken and
battered. Hugo pulls it to him. Clings to it desperately.

                    STATION INSPECTOR
              You demented animal! What were you
              thinking?!

Before Hugo can respond the Station Inspector hauls him away -
- stomping off, cutting through the crowd -- dragging Hugo --
Hugo still clinging to the Automaton--

104   INT. TRAIN STATION -- GRAND HALL - NIGHT   104

They move through the busy Grand Hall. Hugo struggles to free
himself from the Station Inspector.

                    STATION INSPECTOR
              We'll let the orphanage deal with you!

                    HUGO
              No! -- I don't belong there!

                    STATION INSPECTOR
              Where do you belong then? A child has
              to belong to somewhere and to someone!

Hugo finally wrenches himself free. Holds the Automaton to
his chest.

                                                      (CONTINUED)

His emotion is overwhelming. Tears choking him.

> HUGO
> Please ... Please listen to me ...
> You have to let me go ... I don't
> understand ... why my father died
> ... why I'm alone....

He clings to the Automaton.

> HUGO
> This is my only chance ... To work.

He glances at the Station Inspector's leg brace.

> HUGO
> You should understand.

By now a little crowd has formed around them ... Monsieur
Frick ... Madame Emile ... Lisette...

And two new arrivals:

Georges and Isabelle. Georges has heard everything.

> GEORGES
> I do ... I do understand.

He looks at the Station Inspector.

> GEORGES
> Monsieur ... This child belongs to me.

The Station Inspector looks at him.

And then the Station Inspector looks to Lisette. She is
looking back at him. Her eyes imploring him to benevolence.

The Station Inspector smiles. A kind and effortless smile.

And he releases Hugo.

Hugo crosses to Georges and Isabelle.

He still holds the Automaton to him closely:

> HUGO
> I'm sorry ... He's broken...

104   CONTINUED: 104

                          GEORGES
              No he's not ... He worked perfectly.

He embraces Hugo.

And then we see them from high above...

Hugo, Georges, Isabelle, the Automaton...

The train station swirling around them ... Passengers moving
to and fro...

Like the gears and wheels of a clock...

A precise, beautiful machine.

Then we iris down to black.

A title appears:

SIX MONTHS LATER.

We iris back up again to...

The famous man in the moon face from A TRIP TO THE MOON...

105   INT. FILM ACADEMY - THEATRE - NIGHT   105

... Which is painted on the curtain of the impressive Film
Academy theatre.

The theatre is filled with elegant guests. A buzzing crowd. A
gala event.

Hugo, Isabelle and Mama Jeanne sit together.

Hugo has had a haircut. His new, short hair is combed neatly
into place. He is wearing a tuxedo. Very handsome.

He looks almost grown up.

Isabelle, next to him, is bewitching in a formal dress.

The lights dim.

Rene Tabard steps to the stage, in front of the curtain.

                                                      (CONTINUED)

>   TABARD
>   Honored guests, I am proud to welcome
>   you to this gala celebrating the life
>   and work of Georges Melies.

Applause.

Mama Jeanne begins to cry. Isabelle takes her hand.

>   TABARD
>   For years most of his films were
>   thought to be lost. Indeed, Monsieur
>   Melies believed so himself. But we
>   began a search. We looked through
>   vaults and long-forgotten archives,
>   through private collections, barns
>   and catacombs. Our work was rewarded
>   with old negatives, boxes of prints,
>   and trunks full of decaying film,
>   which we were able to save ... We now
>   have over eighty films by Georges
>   Melies!

Applause.

>   TABARD
>   And tonight their creator ... and the
>   newest member of the Film Academy
>   faculty ... is here to share them with
>   you.

He turns and bows.

The magnificent man-in-the-moon curtain parts to reveal...

Georges.

Standing center stage. A movie screen behind him.

His hair and beard have been neatly trimmed. He wears an
elegant tuxedo and looks extremely distinguished.

The audience erupts in cheers and applause.

Finally they are quiet.

>   GEORGES
>   Ladies and gentlemen ... I am standing
>   before you tonight because of one very
>   brave young man...

He finds Hugo's face in the crowd.

> GEORGES
> He saw a broken machine. And against
> all odds, he fixed it ... It was the
> <u>kindest</u> magic trick I have ever seen.

Hugo is moved.

Isabelle looks at him, proud.

> GEORGES
> Now, my friends, I address you all
> tonight as you truly are: wizards,
> mermaids, travelers, adventurers, and
> magicians ... Come and dream with me.

He turns toward the movie screen...

The lights dim...

A flickering projector's light shines...

And we enter the joyous world of Georges Melies.

It is a cornucopia of images from a golden horn. A
phantasmagoria of...

Undersea kingdoms...

Magic tricks...

Wildly dancing devils...

Mysterious submarine journeys...

Gigantic monsters...

Beautiful damsels...

Soaring palaces...

Wondrous balloon voyages...

Knock-about slapstick...

Expanding heads...

Frolicking skeletons...

105 CONTINUED: 105

Lovely star-like angels...

And...

A trip to the moon.

Hugo is barely watching the screen. He is looking at
something else:

Georges stands to the side of the stage, watching.

The glow from the screen illuminates Georges' face.

He is like a man reborn.

Hugo looks at him.

Smiles.

106 INT. APARTMENT - NIGHT   106

A party. After the gala.

The small apartment is crowded with well-wishers and friends.

We float through the party...

Georges is walking down a hallway, talking closely to Rene
Tabard. Film students and other fans crowd around them ...

>   GEORGES
>   ... Honestly, any study of film
>   history must begin with the cave
>   pictographs at Lascaux.

>   TABARD
>   (pleased)
>   You can organize your seminar any
>   way you like, Georges. We're just
>   proud to have you!

>   EAGER STUDENT
>   When can I sign up?

The other students echo this: eager to take Georges' class.

They enter the living room...

                                                    (CONTINUED)

Mama Jeanne sees Georges surrounded by eager students. He
gives her a wink. She winks back then she crosses the room
past...

Monsieur Frick and Madame Emilie sit with Monsieur Labisse.
The dachshunds nuzzle happily on their laps, quite in love...

> MONSIEUR LABISSE
> ... Yes, I think I might have a
> volume on canine socialization. The
> interaction of the breeds is a
> fascinating area of study.

> MONSIEUR FRICK
> (mischieviously)
> Perhaps what we really need is a
> volume on canine <u>romance</u>.

> MADAME EMILIE
> Oh, Monsieur Frick, you are a
> caution.

Then the dachshunds suddenly perk up at the arrival of...

Maximilian ... with the Station Inspector and Lisette, arm-in-
arm. The Station Inspector now wears a shiny, non-squeaking
new leg brace...

> LISETTE
> Remember to smile, dear.

> STATION INSPECTOR
> (smiling)
> It comes more and more easily.

> LISETTE
> (a gentle look)
> I hope so.

He gives her a quick kiss as they cross the room and we
continue on...

To find...

Hugo is dominating a corner of the party, doing wonderful
cards tricks. The crowd around him is impressed.

He glances over, smiles to Isabelle across the room.

She smiles back.

(CONTINUED)

106   CONTINUED: 106

A beat as she watches him.

Then we go with Isabelle as she moves to a quiet corner. She looks over the party for a moment.

Then she sits and begins to write in a notebook.

                  ISABELLE (V.O.)
          Once upon a time, I met a boy named
          Hugo Cabret. He lived in a train
          station...

We move away from Isabelle...

Past Hugo...

Past Georges and Mama Jeanne...

                  ISABELLE (V.O.)
          Why did he live in a train station?
          You might well ask ... That's
          really what this book is going to
          be about...

We move into Hugo's room...

The Automaton, nicely repaired, is watching from a corner.

We go to the Automaton...

                  ISABELLE (V.O.)
          And about how this singular young
          man searched so hard to find a
          secret message from his father...

The Automaton's face...

Looking through the open doorway into the party...

                  ISABELLE (V.O.)
          And how that message lit his way ...
          all the way home.

The Automaton watches Hugo.

You would swear it was smiling.

The End.

PRODUCTION NOTES

Growing up in a section of New York City known as "Little Italy" in the 1940s and '50s, a young Martin Scorsese found a deep connection inside the movie houses of the time—not just to the experience of viewing motion pictures, but also a closeness to his father, who sat with him in the darkened auditorium, fostering the future filmmaker's nascent love of the art form. So when Brian Selznick's award-winning novel *The Invention of Hugo Cabret* landed on his desk via prolific producer Graham King (who had previously collaborated with Scorsese on three films), the Oscar®-winning filmmaker found the tale profoundly resonant. For Scorsese, "It was particularly the vulnerability of a child alone that was striking. Hugo's living in the walls of this giant engine of a sort—the train station—on his own, and he's trying to make that connection with his father, whom he has lost."

Scorsese remembers, "I was given the book about four years ago, and it was one of those experiences…I sat down and read it completely, straight through. There was an immediate connection to the story of the boy, his loneliness, his association with the cinema, with the machinery of creativity. The mechanical objects in the film, including cameras, projectors, and automatons, make it possible for Hugo to reconnect with his father. And mechanical objects make it possible for the filmmaker Georges Méliès to reconnect with his past, and with himself."

Scorsese, in turn, shared the book with his youngest daughter, which only confirmed his belief that the story held a magical quality: "In reading books to my daughter, we re-experience the work. So it's like rediscovering the work of art again, but through the eyes of a child."

Author Brian Selznick recalls the genesis of his book: "At some point I remember seeing *A Trip to the Moon,* the mesmerizing 1902 film by Georges Méliès, and the rocket that flew into the eye of the man in the moon lodged itself firmly in my imagination. I wanted to write a story about a kid who meets Méliès, but I didn't know what the plot would be. The years passed. I wrote and illustrated over 20 other books. Then, sometime in 2003, I happened to pick up a book called *Edison's Eve* by Gaby Wood. It's a history of automatons, and to my surprise, one chapter was about Méliès."

It seems that Méliès' automatons (mechanical figures, powered by inner clockwork, which appear to perform functions on their own) were donated to a museum once the filmmaker passed—they were stored in the attic, where they ended up largely forgotten, ruined by the rain and eventually, thrown away.

Selznick continues, "I instantly imagined a boy climbing through the garbage and finding one of those broken machines. I didn't know who the boy was at first, and I didn't even know his name… I thought the name Hugo sounded kind of French. The only other French word I could think of was *cabaret,* and I thought that Cabret might sound like a real French name. Voila??Hugo Cabret was born."

Research into automatons and clocks, the life of Méliès and the City of Lights in the 1920s and '30s fueled the author's imagination, and the tale of an adventurous boy who lives within the walls of a train station in Paris took life, interwoven with the stories of the colorful characters that surround him. Add in the threads of the discovery of both an abandoned automaton and a largely forgotten filmmaker, and you have Selznick's beautifully illustrated *The Invention of Hugo Cabret (A Novel in Words and Pictures).* Published in 2007, *The Invention of Hugo Cabret (A Novel in Words and Pictures)* won the 2008 Caldecott Medal (awarded by the Association of Library Service to Children to the artist of "the most distinguished American picture book for children") and *The New York Times'* Best Illustrated Book of 2007. It was a number one *New York Times* Bestseller, and a Finalist for the National Book Award.

Producer Graham King: "My producing partner Tim Headington and I were enchanted by Brian Selznick's book. Immediately we thought it would be a beautiful story for Martin Scorsese to create into a piece of cinema."

The team turned to John Logan—their writer on *The Aviator*—to take Selznick's words and illustrations and transform them into a screenplay. As with most book-to-movie conversions, some things had to change. Logan comments, "I had to cut and change some elements of Brian's book to make a more streamlined, shorter movie. The drawings were extremely helpful, because they reminded me of movie storyboards. In effect, they presented a road map for me to follow. In fact, the screenplay opens with a description very similar to Brian's first drawings in the book."

Producer King addresses the perhaps unexpected pairing of Scorsese and the story of Hugo: "All of Scorsese's films have a specific sensibility to them, and *Hugo* is no different. The beautiful imagery and fantastic performances are all there. The main difference is that this film is not made solely for an adult audience—it is for everyone."

To try and replicate the experience of moving through Selznick's work, Scorsese also turned to a different film format. He says, "As moviegoers, we don't have the advantage of the literature, in which you can become aware of Hugo's inner thoughts and feelings. But here, we have his extraordinary face and his actions, and we have 3D. The story needed to be changed to a certain extent, so some elements were dropped from the book. But I think that certain images—particularly in 3D—cover so much territory that the book resonates in them."

Scorsese strove to honor the author's work with every decision, and comments, "Brian Selznick and his book were always an inspiration. We had copies with us all the time. The book has such a distinctive look, whereas our film has its own look and feel, very different from the book, which is in black and white, for one thing. We really went for a blend of realism and a heightened, imagined world."

"IT MIGHT BE AN ADVENTURE": FINDING THE CHARACTERS

When it came time to find the actors who would inhabit the rich array of roles in *Hugo,* Scorsese made an overall decision: "I went with British actors, for the most part to be consistent, and I use the device that the English accent is from the world that they're in. Even though it's Paris 1931, it's a heightened version of that time and place."

Finding the boy to play Hugo was possibly the tallest order to fill. He is the centerpiece of the film, in a majority of the scenes and is somewhere around 12 or 13 years old. With casting director Ellen Lewis, young actors were brought in. Rather early on, Asa Butterfield auditioned for the part. Scorsese remembers, "He read two scenes, and I was convinced immediately. Before making the final decision, I looked at one film, *The Boy in the Striped Pajamas*. Vera [Farmiga] was in the film with him, and I worked with her in *The Departed*. She told me about him, and said he was very, very good."

Almost in the same boat, the young Butterfield didn't really know who Martin Scorsese was, but he had heard good things. Asa says, "I knew who he was, but I hadn't seen any of his films, because most of them are 18's [restricted to 18 and over in Great Britain]. My mum told me that he was the best. When I got the job, everyone said, 'Oh, that's amazing. He's, like, the best director ever!' And so I slowly began to realize how big this actually was. And he **is** the best director. Marty never says 'Do,' instead he encourages you to experiment and says, 'Try this.' And he's such a perfectionist; there are always the slightest changes you can play with. It's been incredible."

Butterfield found the character's inherent mystery to be a big draw. He observes, "You never know that much about him. Loads of traumatic things have happened to him; his father has died; his mother's died. And he ends up living with his Uncle in a train station, doing a man's job. And then his Uncle leaves and doesn't come back. By the time the story starts, all that's happened to him, and he's just left alone with this robotic figure, the automaton. So he's quite to himself until he meets Isabelle, and then that starts getting him out of his shell."

In order to be seen for the role of Isabelle—god-daughter to "Papa Georges" and "Mama Jeanne"—American actress Chloë Grace Moretz adopted a disguise…of sorts. Scorsese recalls her audition: "I was seeing a few young actresses from England. Chloë came in, and she spoke with a British accent, and I thought she was from England as well. At that stage, we started reading actors in pairs for Hugo and Isabelle, and Asa and Chloë just looked right together. There were a couple of other actors, and we switched the pairs, but the looks weren't right. Not only did they look right together, they sounded right together. They play off of each other very well, and they have very distinctive personalities, very different."

Moretz also recalls: "I met him for the first time in New York, and it was actually the first time I set foot in New York since I started in this business. So it was a really cool turn of events, because I show up in New York for the first time in seven years and I am meeting Martin Scorsese for this phenomenal role. I went in and met him, and he was just really warm. He told me a bunch of stories and I thought, 'Wow, he's a really cool guy.'"

Chloë was also attracted to the mystery aspect of the story, but more in the external sense. "Being 13 years old, as the characters are, there's always something that you want to find out. There's always something that you're poking and prying, trying to figure out what's going on, or how something works. In this movie, Isabelle and Hugo are poking and prying at people."

As far as having his two younger leads putting on a "period" style, the director had a firm notion—don't do it. He offers, "We don't put up a title card that says "1931." It doesn't matter, because what the children are, what they need, what they're looking for, how they behave, it's contemporary, it's universal, it's not something of a time and place. It's something that is natural, and therefore, it doesn't matter what time this film takes place. And the children simply behave like children."

For the key role of Georges Méliès, "Papa Georges," the director/producer didn't have to look very far in any direction. Per Scorsese: "I've always wanted to work with Ben Kingsley over the years, and finally I got these two pictures, *Shutter Island*—we had a really good working relationship on that picture—and now, this. He's an extraordinary actor, really one of the greats, which I don't even need to say…just look at his body of work. His range, his versatility. In any event, when we looked at the image of Georges Méliès, there was no doubt in my mind that the look would be perfect for Ben."

The look, yes, but what mattered even more to Kingsley was the physicality of this man in decline. Scorsese was amazed at the performer's exacting technique: "Ben worked out a way of moving, with a sense of defeat…a defeated impression of his body, a defeated posture. This, after the man had been so alive, making 500 films, three films a week, doing magic shows in the evening, and having to shoot during the daytime. He created a whole new art form and suddenly, he loses all of his money, has to burn everything and winds up sitting behind the counter of a toy store in a very quiet part of the Gare Montparnasse."

In Kingsley's research, he found much to admire on a personal basis in Méliès, beyond the man's visionary talent in cinema. The actor relates, "Georges had the confidence and charisma of a great stage magician. He had to be very precise in the execution of his tricks—sawing people in half, levitations, disappearances, that sort of thing—and his sleight of hand. His precision was contagious to his cast and crew. Given that he made hundreds of films, they must have been very disciplined indeed. He ran a tight ship, but I hear he ran it very affectionately. He rarely lost his temper or raised his voice, if ever. He had a way of gently reminding people what they'd forgotten to do, reminding them when he had said something before. What a man he must have been."

Just as his character shifts from magic to cinema, Kingsley sees a natural evolution in Martin Scorsese's venture into 3D filmmaking: "I suppose it's a little bit like an artist going from fine portrait painting to landscape painting. It's a shift in the way he puts his brush, but it's the same brush and it's the same canvas."

A looming presence in the train station and the constant threat to Hugo's independent way of life is the Station Inspector, a role slightly modified from the novel. Per Scorsese: "We asked Brian Selznick if we could open up this part, because I just didn't want it to be a figure of fear—basically, a villain, just to threaten and catch the boy. I wanted him to have a little more flavor, more levels to him, and so I thought by working with Sacha Baron Cohen we could find that."

Baron Cohen describes his take on his character: "Now naturally, in any train station, it's dangerous for children to be running around. So in the '20s and '30s, with the working conditions and such, if you have homeless children about, unsupervised, it would present a danger to the passengers and the kids themselves. So, you have me, a Station Inspector. He's this wonderful fellow who's utterly repulsive and horrid to children, but yet, there's a different side to him. He has a gentler side. He was probably in an orphanage himself, and he is actually a war invalid. He's limited physically by a metallic attachment to his leg, which we imply may have been the result of a war wound, but it was most likely self-inflicted, by accident."

Inadvertently, the actor had already begun his own research in the physical style of comedy of the day: "In England, I think Harold Lloyd was on television everyday after school, so we kind of grew up watching him. I never found him that funny at the time, but there are references in *Hugo* to those films, particularly *Safety Last,* where he climbs up a building, and does this incredible stunt and gets stuck on a clock that falls backwards. We directly reference that. So Martin wanted me to look at these early comedians, which was very interesting. They were doing brilliant stuff, people like Keaton and Chaplin. Yeah, I discovered this very obscure guy called Charles Chaplin, I believe, and his work is quite interesting—definitely worth a look."

Scorsese also came up with another way to add facets to the "villain" of the piece. Baron Cohen explains, "When Marty and I met originally, we were talking about ways to make the villain not seem like an archetypal villain—Marty had this idea of bringing in some romance. And it was quite lovely to have Emily Mortimer, who is a wonderful actress and woman, play my love interest, so there is a bit of love. You know, the Inspector really is a nasty man. He's a horrible man, but deep down, he is a nice guy. It's just really deep…down."

Scorsese expresses, "Emily is one of the best actors around, she has a great sense of humor, and she was a wonderful choice to play a love interest for Sacha, which was unique for him to try."

The Station Inspector isn't the only threat to Hugo. He is brought to live in the train station, in fact, by his estranged Uncle Claude, a menacing lout who promptly pawns off his maintenance duties onto the small boy.

The director/producer: "I worked with Ray Winstone in *The Departed,* which was a great experience. Ray has this passive menace—he doesn't need to be involved in any dialogue or anything physical, but you can still feel this darkness lurking in his character. I thought he would bring that threatening gravity to Hugo's Uncle Claude."

Perhaps even more than performing in the role, Winstone enjoyed the shared experience of working with Scorsese in 3D. Ray says, "The joy for me during filming was actually watching Scorsese work, because it was like he was falling in love with making a film again. Watching him with 3D, with something he'd never worked with before . . . it was like watching a kid with a new toy. And the feeling was palpable and eventually passed around the cast and crew."

For the key featured role of Hugo's father, Scorsese needed to find an actor who could embody all of the warmth and goodness that the young boy had experienced (up to that point in his life) in just a few short scenes.

"I worked with Jude Law once before, when he played Errol Flynn in *The Aviator.* I also saw him onstage as Hamlet, and he was really wonderful. He's so unique. He has the authority and the charm for this part, and I'd love to be able to work with him in a longer project," offers Scorsese.

Law professes, "I knew the book because I'd already read it to my children. So I went back and re-read it, and I talked to my children about it and asked them their impressions of the father. I got to talk to a clockmaker, and I looked at automatons, so I had a certain knowledge of how to hold things, and if they were referring to tools, I'd know what they were. But otherwise, to me, really, it was simply about creating a very warm and heartfelt chapter in Hugo's life, knowing that the majority of the story sets him in quite a cold world. I wanted to make sure that you realize he had been loved. I thought it was really important that I carry my experiences of being a father into it."

For the role of Monsieur Labisse, who runs a book shop in the train station, Scorsese finally had the opportunity to work with a truly legendary performer. He states, "On this film I finally got the chance to work with Christopher Lee, who's been a favorite of mine for 50, 60 years."

The 89-year-old Lee recalls traveling in France in 1931: "I remember very well those shops, cafés, and restaurants. So to me, in a way, it's like stepping into my past. My character is sort of a guardian angel, and I help open the world to these children through literature."

Lee was thrilled to finally be able to cross Martin Scorsese off of his list: "Not to flatter Martin, but I said to him, 'I have more credits probably than anyone in the industry alive today, so I'm told. But I always felt that my career would not be absolutely complete unless I did a film with you, because I've worked with John Huston, Orson Welles, Raoul Walsh, Steven Spielberg, Tim Burton, Peter Jackson and many, many, many, many others, but never with you.' Along comes this story, and obviously there is something for me. So finally!"

Scorsese cast Helen McCrory in the pivotal role of Madame Jeanne, the support and protector of the aging Méliès, who at one time was his muse. Scorsese explains, "I had seen Helen in *The Queen* as Mrs. Blair, and in a British television series of *Anna Karenina,* and she was excellent. We got to meet, talked, and I thought she would be perfect for the role. It's a complex situation: Madame Jeanne, who supports her husband, has worked with him for years and wants him to get past the bitterness of his great disappointment in life. She was wonderful, working in different layers, shades and colors into her performance."

The crucial role of René Tabard, the film scholar who, thanks to Hugo and Isabelle, rediscovers Méliès and arranges the gala in his honor at the French Film Academy, went to the versatile screen and stage actor Michael Stuhlbarg. Scorsese was delighted at being reunited with him. "This is the third time Michael and I have worked together. He appeared in the commercial for Freixenet champagne I shot that was an homage to Alfred Hitchcock, and he also played a leading role in *Boardwalk Empire.* Michael's range as an actor is astonishing. He can switch effortlessly from drama to comedy, from a contemporary film to a period piece. He's equally brilliant as a vicious, hardened crime boss in *Boardwalk* or, in *Hugo,* as a gentle, self-effacing film historian who idolizes George Méliès and is in awe of his movies. It was a great pleasure working with Michael again."

A great deal of the "local color" of the train station is provided by people who depend upon the traffic in the station's main hall for their livelihood, which include the flowerseller, Lisette (Mortimer); the bookseller, Labisse (Lee); a gentleman who runs the newsstand, Monsieur Frick; and his neighbor, who runs the café, Madame Emilie. For the role of the slightly eccentric (potential) couple, Scorsese slotted two of Great Britain's finest character actors, Richard Griffiths ("one of the greatest actors working today," states Scorsese) and Frances de la Tour ("I've always been a great admirer of hers," he adds).

The director elaborates, "The characters that John Logan placed in this little world of the station, in our impression of Paris at that time, I call them the 'vignettes'; they inhabit this world. They work there everyday. All these characters were meant to weave in and out of the picture, with everybody trying to connect with each other, the way Hugo is trying to connect with his past."

Scorsese approached the vignettes with a light touch, and shot them almost like a silent film. The characters quietly, almost wordlessly, move in and out of frame as they relate to each other. Just watching them, scenarios arise, which add to the atmosphere and the feel of the train station.

As the Station Inspector's menacing dog, Maximillian, three trained Dobermans were brought in (Blackie was used in most scenes, with Enzo and Borsalino in the wings to cover). Trainer Mathilde de Cagny also oversaw the use of the longhaired dachshunds (which play into the story of Frick and Emilie), a cat (forever perched atop a pile of books in Labisse's shop) and several pigeons (what's a clocktower without pigeons?). De Cagny herself was usually costumed and stationed in the crowd, near enough to the action to "direct" the animals, but not evident enough to pull focus and spoil the shot. When no crowds were present, she was outfitted in a "green screen" suit, for easy removal in post-production.

To fill the role of one very special character—who is central to the plot and its unfolding—filmmakers turned to props master David Balfour, who worked with
"problem-solving" prop builder Dick George, creator of Hugo's automaton.

Dick George offers, "He's a character in himself, so in a way, it's like building a little human being." A total of 15 automatons were built for filming, each one, to execute a different move or serve a different purpose within the script.

George continues, "The advantage that we have in manufacturing this piece is that we have all modern technologies at our disposal, which early clockmakers didn't have. However, they had a wealth of experience and understanding of clockwork mechanisms. The early automatons were driven on a cam system, and the information was programmed in, letter-by-letter, so the amount that it could actually write or draw was quite limited. In our case, because it's a computer program, it can draw absolutely anything."

Of his taciturn co-star, Asa Butterfield notes, "It's really odd. It does feel like he's another actor. When I heard that I was going to be working with a robot for a portion of this movie, I thought it might look like the Tin Man from *The Wizard of Oz*, but it looks so human."

Ben Kingsley observes, "The automaton took on a life of its own. It was very touching and beautiful to watch the little chap turn his head, dip his pen into a pot of ink and draw the face of the moon, which I watched it do with my own eyes. There was one scene, where Hugo comes to Georges while cradling the automaton, which really is a child holding a lost child. Then I take the little chap in my arms, and we walk off—and then it's really three children walking away."

"SEEING DREAMS IN THE MIDDLE OF THE DAY": FINDING THE REAL MÉLIÈS

"I had a DVD set, of course, of Méliès films, and there's an image of Méliès on the cover," Scorsese says. "One day on the set, two of the kids in the movie went by, both about 12 years old. One saw the DVD box and said, 'Oh, there's Ben (Kingsley),' I responded, 'No, that's really Méliès.' 'You mean he existed, he's real?' I said, 'Oh, yes.'"

Georges Méliès was not the first to make films—that honor belongs to two brothers, Auguste and Louis Lumière, who invented "moving pictures" in 1895 and went on to make hundreds of films, mostly documenting "real-life" events (e.g., one of their first, *L'Arrivée d'un train á La Ciotat,* had early cinemagoers literally jumping out of their seats as a huge steam engine raced through the frame). The story goes that the brothers, however, believed this new pastime to be literally a passing fancy.

Georges Méliès thought otherwise. Eschewing the family business of shoemaking, Méliès sold the factory and took the proceeds to fund the beginning of his chosen profession—magic. He purchased a theater (formerly owned by his mentor, Jean-Eugène Robert-Houdin, the magician who inspired the young Ehrich Weiss to change his name to Harry Houdini) and began performing.

He saw his first moving picture when he was 34 and to him, this new art form held great promise…for magic. He constructed his own cameras and projectors, with the help of R. W. Paul, oftentimes repurposing parts from a collection of automatons Robert-Houdin had left behind. His earliest films re-created his stage performances. However, he soon began to experiment with storytelling and editing techniques, giving rise to some of the earliest cinematic "special effects," including stop motion, time-lapse photography, multiple exposures and dissolves, and hand-painted colors. He later sold his theater and built his studio, with a stage entirely of glass (to best utilize all available light) at its heart.

"What's amazing about Méliès," offers Scorsese, "is that he explored and invented pretty much everything that we're doing now. It is in a direct line, all the way, from the sci-fi and fantasy films of the '30s, '40s and '50s, up to the work of Harryhausen, Spielberg, Lucas, James Cameron. It's all there. Méliès did what we do now with computer, green screen and digital, only he did it in his camera at his studio."

His "masterpiece," the 14-minute *Le voyage dans la lune (A Trip to the Moon)*, was filmed in 1902. He went on to write, direct, act in, produce, and design more than 500 films by 1914, with subjects ranging from "reality" (re-creations of current events) to fantasy/sci-fi (from *Kingdom of the Fairies* to *The Impossible Voyage*), with playing times from one to 40 minutes in length. Méliès is often referred to as the "Father of Narrative Filmmaking," with many crediting him with the birth of the fantasy, science fiction, and horror genres.

Because of an unfortunate incident with Thomas Alva Edison (who acquired a print of Méliès' 1896 *The House of Devil,* duplicated and exhibited it in the U.S. with great success…without giving any profits to Méliès), the filmmaker began to film two prints simultaneously, one for European and one for American exhibition. Recently, a film historian combined both prints of *The Infernal Cake Walk* and found the resulting image to be a crude precursor to 3D cinema.

Advances in the art of cinema later left Méliès behind, and with the outbreak of World War I, he saw his appeal waning. He eventually abandoned his studio, burned his costumes and sets, and sold the copies of his films to be melted down for chemical use.

To support himself, his second wife, and his granddaughter, Méliès worked in a confectionery and toy booth seven days a week at one of Paris' central train stations, Gare Montparnasse, in the 1920s. He remained largely forgotten until the artistic community of French Surrealists "discovered" his work, connecting with his dreamlike vision. Renewed interest led to a gala in Paris, with Méliès front and center, screening many of his works. He was even working on a new film, *The Ghosts of the Metro*, when he died in 1938.

Scorsese remarks, "When I first read the book, I didn't realize that the older gentleman in the toy store was going to turn out to be Georges

Méliès. It's a true story. He was broke, and did wind up in a toy store at the Gare Montparnasse for 16 years."

Ben Kingsley explains, "The fictionalizing is discreet in our film. It was believed by many that Georges died around about the time of the First World War, but he actually isolated himself in his shop. It's been re-created, wonderfully, from photographs and from people who were close to him. The nudge of history is delicate and charming."

BALANCING REALISM AND MYTH: SCORSESE'S PARIS OF 1931

To re-create the world of Paris in the early '30s, as filtered through Hugo Cabret, a fictional character, Scorsese aimed to create, as he put it, "a balance of realism and myth." He brought researcher Marianne Bower onboard, who looked to lend authenticity, supported by historical photographs, documents, and films of the period. She narrowed her search to isolate the time period of 1925 to 1931.

As a course of study for the creative departments, members of Team Hugo watched about 180 of Mélies' films, about 13 hours' worth, along with films of René Clair and Carol Reed, avant-garde cinema from the 1920s and '30s. They watched films of the Lumière brothers, and silent films from the '20s to study period tinting and toning. Reference was not limited to "moving pictures," as they also studied still photography of Brassaï (Hungarian photographer Gyula K. Halász, who memorialized Paris between the Wars) for the period look of the Parisian streets and the appearance and behavior of the background actors.

While some location filming would take place, the majority of filming was to be done at England's Shepperton Studios, where the production designer Dante Ferretti would supervise the construction of Hugo's world, which included a life-size train station with all of its shops, Mélies' entire apartment building, his glass studio building, a bombed-out structure next door, a fully stocked corner wine shop and an enormous graveyard marked by huge monuments and stone crypts, among others.

The centerpiece of the tale, the station, was an amalgamation of design elements and structures lifted from multiple train stations of the period—some still in existence, which proved helpful to many of the artists; sadly, Gare

Montparnasse was destroyed and rebuilt anew in 1969. Per Scorsese, "Our station is a combination of several different train stations in Paris at that time. Also, our Paris is really a heightened Paris…our impression of Paris at the time."

Ferretti's impressive sets were brought even more into the period with the help of set decorator Francesca Lo Schiavo, who joyfully admits that she had the pitiable task of repeated shopping trips to flea markets in and around Paris. She also supervised the reproduction of posters from 1930-31 for use in the station and on some building exteriors. Some design elements were also inspired references to some of the best of French cinema.

An experience from Ferretti's youth also proved quite useful to the designer—at age eight, the father of his best friend worked with clocks, and once he began to incorporate them into his designs, "all my memory about this came back…I had forgotten everything." (The actual construction of the clocks themselves was done by Joss Williams of special effects.)

When finished, the main hall of the train station filled a soundstage, running 150 feet in length, 120 in width and 41 in height. The overwhelmingly immersive environment allowed Scorsese and director of photography Robert Richardson to film all the movement, bustle and collision of the multiple stories dictated in Logan's screenplay, including a rather breathless chase between the Station Inspector and Hugo.

Costume designer Sandy Powell also looked to the past for information and inspiration, but also, played fully with the idea of Scorsese's "impression of Paris" agenda. Vintage clothing figured heavily—for reference and for actual use—but for those actually worn by an actor, they had to be subjected to strengthening (at the very least) or even re-made.

Powell found Hugo's signature striped sweater, then had copies made (several sets of identical costumes were necessary for characters who appear in largely unchanged outfits throughout the film). When Helen McCrory appears as a constellation in one of Méliès' films, she was outfitted in a found skirt (from an old costume or ball gown from the '40s or '50s, Powell surmises), which, with added bodice, was refashioned into the airy costume befitting a "star." Kingsley's costumes as Méliès were taken directly from photographs, then padded, to not only give the actor a more slumped silhouette, but also to remind him not to stand up straight.

But history did not always have the final say—for the Station Inspector's uniform, Powell rejected the bottle green color called for in favor of a near-turquoise blue.

"IT'S A PUZZLE—WHEN YOU PUT IT TOGETHER, SOMETHING'S GOING TO HAPPEN": FILMING HUGO'S WORLD IN 3D

Martin Scorsese is not shy about professing his affection for 3D filmmaking, having spent his formative years attending the cinema at the same time that 3D was being utilized for films across every genre. He says, "It was 1953, and the first one I saw was *House of Wax,* directed by André de Toth—it's probably the best 3D film ever made."

It was, however, a film released the following year that Scorsese cites as having a truly lasting effect on the argument for a "smart use" of 3D in service to the story. He offers, "Alfred Hitchcock's use of 3D in *Dial M for Murder* was really intelligent. Rather than as an effect, it deals with the story, and it utilizes space as an element in the narrative. What I discovered working in 3D is that it enhances the actor, like watching a sculpture that moves. It's no longer flat. With the right performances and the right moves, it becomes a mixture of theater and film, but different from both. That is something that has always been exciting to me…I've always dreamed about doing a film in 3D."

As part of a primer in 3D filmmaking, crew members were shown both *House of Wax* and *Dial M for Murder.* For Scorsese's cinematographer, Robert Richardson, it was also the first time working in the format. Per the director/producer: "Bob's a wonderful artist, and he had never done 3D, so we were always pushing each other. We wanted to try it, and so we were both discovering more about it as we went along.

"Probably the first images I saw in my head when I began working on *Hugo,*" continues Scorsese, "were images of Hugo running and looking over his shoulder, and there was this longing in his eyes. Faces are given a special intimacy with 3D. We see people in a different way. They are closer to us. I felt that 3D would help create a stronger bond between the audience and the characters."

Robert Richardson states, "*Hugo* provided an unparalleled challenge. My hope was to evoke the romance of Paris in the 1930's and yet not divorce the present. French cinema has always had a special place in my heart and with the vast potential of 3D, I hoped to sample the magic with which Méliès created his body of work."

To help with the challenges of filming in an added dimension, 3D stereographer Demetri Portelli was hired. During shooting, he could always be found working from a special monitor, using a remote control to adjust each camera's "eye" on the 3D rig. Portelli elaborates, "3D enhances the viewing experience. It creates a physical world closer to reality than ever before, intensifying the audience's involvement in the story."

For the scene where Hugo and Isabelle venture to the library, location filming took place at the Bibliothèque Sainte-Geneviève. Richardson had prepared lighting cranes outside the windows to simulate sunshine, but when it was time to film, the sun came cascading into the voluminous library, one window at a time. Portelli describes, "Some atmosphere was added with a white smoke, so we could define the rays of light. On my 3D screen, they looked like solid beams of platinum. In my experience this can only be achieved by shooting in 3D. Filming native 3D—capturing 3D on set with a motorized rig—I can move each camera's lens around an object from two different positions, like the eyes in your head 'see' from different angles. This process enables us to build objects with volume and gives all the images in the film a wonderful physical tangibility."

The air of the train station received similar treatment—to give viewers the impression of the age and feel of the place. "Dust" was created from tiny bits of goose down, and dry ice "smoke" was also added.

Hugo was also the 3D maiden voyage of the film's editor, Thelma Schoonmaker, who felt the format a rich addition to the project. She says, "Scorsese's and Richardson's use of 3D in *Hugo* seems to embrace the actors. It has a powerful effect on the emotion in the film."

But *Hugo* is about more than an adventurous boy on a hopeful mission—it is also about the discovery and reaffirmation of a true artist of early cinema. In flashback, audiences are shown the entire arc of Méliès' career...from magician to filmmaker and then, shopkeeper. Scenes of him actually filming are key. As he is credited with more than 500 films, Scorsese faced the challenge of winnowing down such a lengthy list of movie titles to just a handful. Finally, he chose the one for the full "behind-the-scenes" treatment—his 1903 *Kingdom of the Fairies*. Per Scorsese: "I wanted to show three or four scenes from it, but actually I wound up with one that takes place under the sea. We thought that would be interesting to show how he accomplished his underwater sequences—how simple it is, and how charming."

Méliès' original glass studio was rebuilt on the backlot of Shepperton Studios in England, constructed from existing designs, measurements, and photos of the original building. Cinémathèque Française provided Méliès' diagram for filming "underwater"—Scorsese's team could re-create the placement of the fish tank and the camera in order to reproduce Méliès' effect.

Visual effects supervisor Rob Legato was charged with figuring out how to achieve the litany of filmic effects Méliès first created using only the available tools and techniques of the time. Legato offers, "This was a magic project, having the opportunity to go back to the very beginnings of the film business with someone like Marty at the helm. To a large degree, what I do in my profession is visual effects, and here is essentially the 'father of visual effects.' He created this in-camera trickery and had such love for the art form— it's so much a part of this movie."

Scorsese also features more of Méliès' work as "films within the film," such as *A Thousand and One Nights,* which features a group of dancing skeletons that appear to vanish when confronted by sword-wielding adventurers. The filmmaker himself appeared as Satan in multiple projects, and Kingsley appears in perfect imitation, down to the costume and the "disappearance" through a trap door in the floor. Other scenes are representative of several similar ones from multiple films, and the dragon is one such multi-sourced creation.

Whenever any Méliès film was "directly" quoted onscreen by Scorsese, hours of work went in to authentically reproducing every aspect of the film— from the appearances of the performers and their movements, to the costumes, lighting, and effects. Footage was re-created frame by frame, in painstaking detail. Legato confirms, "I can't describe enough the lengths to which we went to create the spirit of Méliès in his studio—the costumes, the makeup, the lighting, the assistant directors working out the blocking and expressions of the actors exactly as they looked in the original films. It's as accurate as we could get matching the clips, beat for beat."

Authenticity and accuracy were indeed the mandate, and filmmakers went above and beyond to keep the vision "true"…for example, the period seamstresses shown working on Georges Méliès' films are actually the crew seamstresses from *Hugo*. Scorsese confesses, "It was an enormous undertaking, and we didn't fully realize how challenging it would be. But it was enjoyable. We really felt, when we were working in the Méliès Studio, that it was a celebration for all of us and an honor to be making our versions of these lasting works."

While Kingsley was duly inspired from watching all of the existing films of Méliès, he found a more direct character inspiration much nearer to hand: "I watched all of Georges' films, but it's not a question for me of preparation and research. That's minimal. It doesn't really teach you anything about what it's like to be Georges. But then, working with Marty, who is such a genius, I realized that my role model for playing Georges Méliès should be Martin Scorsese! There he is. Why look any further? I didn't have to go out and research someone who's been dead for a long time, I can't speak with him. I feel I'm living with a pioneer of cinema, in the same room, day after day. That's where I looked."

Méliès created his effects using trial and error—filming, waiting for the film to be developed and edited, then viewing it…it either worked or it didn't. Legato turned to "tried and true" techniques to achieve onscreen magic for Scorsese, especially with one massive scene involving a derailed locomotive that screeches through the station and explodes out of one of the gigantic windows into the Paris street below.

Just such an accident occurred at the Gare Montparnasse, on October 23, 1895. The still shocking image of the train engine in the street, the back end leaning up against the remains of the grand window, became Legato's reference. He explains, "My first instinct was to photograph the scene. I had very good experiences photographing miniature models in *Titanic* and *Apollo 13*. So, we constructed the train and the window [in 1:4 scale], set up the same mechanics, and it reacted much like it did when the historical crash really occurred, and ultimately, matching the train's twisted position just like in the photograph."

Construction of the 15-foot-long train and 20-foot-tall station window took the design team and engineers four months to build. To achieve additional scale, models of miniature bicycles and suitcases were added to the street just below the window. The actual model train crash took only a second-and-a-half, but when slowed down and finished off with other effects, the result is in scale and quite convincing.

For a few scenes, Scorsese took his 3D camera on location, to add even more period feel and authenticity. Scenes with Jude Law as Hugo's father, working at his museum job, London's internationally renowned Victoria and Albert Museum stood in for a Parisian one. Isabelle and Hugo go to the cinema in a historic film house in Paris—an actual one—the lobby decorated with existing antique posters from silent films and films in release in 1930 and '31. The Parisian theater where Georges is feted is, in fact, a lecture hall at the Sorbonne—the historical landmark in the Latin Quarter, the 5th arrondissement of Paris, which formerly housed the centuries' old center of learning. A younger Georges is shown levitating Jeanne in a flashback, and the sequence was filmed at the Athénée Théâtre Louis-Jouvet in Paris (the look of the scene was inspired by a period poster advertising the illusion, even down to Sandy Powell hand-painting the inside of Jeanne's skirt, which is visible while the damsel is floating).

Paris, France, in 1931 is evident in every aspect of *Hugo,* from the costumes, to the sets, the dressing and the styling. Composer Howard Shore's score is a love letter, both to the French culture in the 1930s and to the groundbreaking early days of cinema. Shore's music is composed for two ensembles—one nested within the other—to create a sense of layering in the musical palette. Inside a full symphony orchestra resides a smaller ensemble, a sort of nimble French dance band that includes the ondes Martenot, musette, cimbalom, tack piano, gypsy guitar, upright bass, a 1930s trap-kit, and alto saxophone. "I wanted to match the depth of the sound to the depth of the image—a marriage of light and sound," says Shore.

"LEADING ALL THE WAY HOME": LA FIN D'UN REVE

For Ben Kingsley, bringing the "Father of Narrative Filmmaking" to life was only one of the benefits of performing in *Hugo.* Kingsley posits, "The characters are so rich, and the actors playing them so gifted, they really have found the joy, the glory and the surprise that one usually finds in an animated film. But it goes far beyond that—Martin has used the natural eccentricities and energies of the performers to great effect. It's got mystery, it's funny and moving. The set is breathtakingly beautiful; the toys in my shop are exquisite. The colors, the 3D…it's terribly entertaining, and wonderful in the most literal sense."

From first seeing *A Trip to the Moon,* to watching his illustrated novel transformed into a film, author Brian Selznick maintained his gratitude and sense of wonder: "Watching the movie now, I think about myself as a child drawing day and night, and I think about Martin Scorsese in the cinema with his father, and Thelma Schoonmaker growing up in Aruba, and John Logan watching Laurence Olivier as Hamlet, and Dante Ferretti sitting in a clock tower in Italy. I marvel at the long, unexpected twists and turns that led us here…children from all over the world who grew up and came together to collaborate on a movie about two lonely kids who find their purpose in a train station in Paris."

Scorsese closes, "As a moviemaker, I feel that everything done in film today began with Georges Méliès. And when I go back and look at his original films, I feel moved and inspired, because they still carry the thrill of discovery over 100 years after they were made; and because they are among the first, powerful expressions of an art form that I've loved, and to which I've devoted myself for the better part of my life."

CAST AND CREW CREDITS

PARAMOUNT PICTURES AND GK FILMS PRESENT
A GK FILMS/INFITUM NIHIL PRODUCTION
BEN KINGSLEY SASHA BARON COHEN ASA BUTTERFIELD CHLOE GRACE MORETZ

"HUGO"

RAY WINSTONE EMILY MORTIMER AND JUDE LAW

Directed by
MARTIN SCORESE

Screenplay by
JOHN LOGAN

Based on the book entitled
"The Invention of Hugo Cabret"
by BRIAN SELZNICK

Produced by
GRAHAM KING
TIM HEADINGTON
MARTIN SCORSESE
JOHNNY DEPP

Executive Producers
EMMA TILLINGER KOSKOFF
DAVID CROKETT
GEORGIA KACANDES
CHRISTI DEMBROWSKI
BARBARA DEFINA

Director of Photography
ROBERT RICHARDSON, ASC

Editor
THELMA SCHOONMAKER

Production Designed by
DANTE FERRETTI

Costume Designer
SANDY POWELL

Visual Effects Supervisor
ROB LEGATO

Music Supervisor
RANDALL POSTER

Composer
HOWARD SHORE

Casting
ELLEN LEWIS

Hair & Make-Up Designer
DANIEL PARKER

Production Sound Mixer
RAY BECKETT, CAS

CAST

Georges Méliès	Ben Kingsley
Station Inspector	Sacha Baron Cohen
Hugo Cabret	Asa Butterfield
Isabelle	Chlofi Grace Moretz
Uncle Claude	Ray Winstone
Lisette	Emily Mortimer
Monsieur Labisse	Christopher Lee
Mama Jeanne	Helen McCrory
Rene Tabard	Michael Stuhlbarg
Madame Emilie	Frances de la Tour
Monsieur Frick	Richard Griffiths
Hugo's Father	Jude Law
Policeman	Kevin Eldon
Young Tabard	Gulliver McGrath
Street Kid	Shaun Aylward
Django Reinhardt	Emil Lager
Theatre Manager	Angus Barnett
Camera Technician	Edmund Kingsley
Train Engineer	Max Wrottesley
Train Engineer Assistant	Marco Aponte
Café Waitress	Ilona Cheshire
Children at Café	Francesca Scorsese
	Emily Surgent
	Lily Carlson

Arabian Knights	Frederick Warder
	Chrisos Lawson
	Tomos James
Young Tabard's Brother	Ed Sanders
Circus Barkers	Terence Frisch
	Max Cane
Gendarmes	Frank Bourke
	Stephen Box
Salvador Dali	Ben Addis
James Joyce	Robert Gill

CREW

Unit Production Managers	Charles Newirth
	Georgia Kacandes
	Angus More Gordon
First Assistant Director	Chris Surgent
Second Assistant Director	Richard Graysmark
Stunt Coordinator	Doug Coleman
Assistant Stunt Coordinator	Richard Bradshaw
Hugo Stunt Doubles	Scott Hutchison
	Edward Upcott
Isabelle Stunt Double	Talila Craig
Mama Jeanne Stunt Double	Dani Biernat
Monsieur Frick Stunt Double	Steve Emerson
Supervising Art Director	David Warren

Set Decorator . . . . Francesca Lo Schiavo
Property Master. . . . . David Balfour
Art Directors . . . . Rod McLean
    Luca Tranchino   Christian Huband
    Stuart Rose   Martin Foley
Production Controller . . . . Emma Bendell
Production Coordinator . . . . Hannah Godwin
First Assistant "A" Camera . . . Gregor Tavenner
"B" Camera Operator / Steadicam
. . . . Larry McConkey
First Assistant "B" Camera / Systems Tech
. . . . Olly Tellett
Second Assistant "A" Camera . . . . Tash Gamper
Second Assistant "B" Camera . . . Dora Krolikowska
Third Assistant Camera . . . . . Megan Ogilvie
Camera Trainee. . . . . Jessica Greene
3D Stereographer . . . . Demetri Portelli
3D Camera Systems Engineer . . . . Ben Gervais
    Tom Mitchell
Production Sound Mixer . . . . . John Midgley
Sound Maintenance . . . . Mike Reardon
Cable Person. . . . . Charlotte Gray
Video Assist Operator . . . . Ian Kelly
Assistant Video Assist Operator . . . Luke Haddock
Chief Lighting Technician . . . . . Ian Kincaid
Gaffer . . . . Lee Walters
Rigging Gaffer . . . . Gavin Walters
Best Boys. . . . . Paul Sharp
    Steve Kitchen
Floor Electricians. . . . . Terry Roberts
    Emily Plant   Mark Thomas
    Andrew Nolan   Adrian Mackay
    Ross Busby
Desk Operator . . . . Jason Fletcher
Key Grip . . . . Chris Centrella
Key Grip UK . . . . Malcolm Huse
Dolly Grip . . . . Pat Garrett
Crane Technicians . . . . Neil Tomlin
    Ben Edwards
Head Technician . . . . Steve Hideg
Lighting Grip – Best Boy . . . Howard Davidson
Lighting Grips   Peter Harris
    Paul Harris   Lee Eldred
    Toby Tyler   Paul Brown
Chargehand Rigging Electricians . . . Larry Park
    Jimmy Harris
Rigging Electricians . . . . Andy Purdy
    Daniel Walters   Andy Green
    Adam Harris   Mark Joiner
Dimmer Technician . . . . Peter Davies
HOD Electrical Rigger . . . . . . Richard Harris
Supervising Electrical Rigger . . . Robert Clarke
Chargehand Electrical Riggers . . . . James Busby
    Glenn Prescott   Robert Owen

Electrical Riggers . . . . Rikki Harris
    Steve Macher   Andy Watson
    John Robertson   Garry Ridgwell
    Gary Evans
Standby Electrical Riggers . . . . . Mick Heath
    Aaron Montgomery
Re-Recording Mixer . . Tom Fleischman, C.A.S.
Supervising Sound Editors . . . . Philip Stockton
    Eugene Gearty
Music Editor. . . . . Jennifer Dunnington
Associate Editor . . . . Scott Brock
VFX Editor . . . . Red Charyszyn
Special Effects Supervisor . . . . . Joss Williams
Special Effects Coordinator / Buyer
. . . . Andrea Williams
Special Effects Assistant Coordinator
. . . . Jess Lewington
Special Effects Supervisor's Assistant . . Ashley Yallop
Lead Senior Special Effects Tech . . David Watson
Special Effects Techs . . . . . . Hayley Williams
    David McGeary   Stuart Prior
    Freddie Joe Farnsworth
Assistant Special Effects Tech . . . . . Chris Giles
Special Effects Workshop Supervisor Stuart Digby
Lead Senior Special Effects Workshop Tech
. . . . Tony Edwards
Senior Special Effects Workshop Techs
. . . . Andy Bunce
    Michael Durkan   Steve Lloyd
Special Effects Workshop Techs . . Mark Holdcroft
    Frederick Buhagiar   Mick Booys
Special Effects Workshop Assistant Techs . . . . .
    Andy Ryan   Derek Jones
Special Effects PAs . . Tom McLoughlin, Tom Lloyd
Lead Senior Rigging Special Effects Tech
. . . . Andy Willliams
Senior Rigging Special Effects Tech . . Shaun Rutter
Breakaway Senior Special Effects Technician
. . . . Keith Shannon
Location Property Master . . . . . . John Wells
Property Supervisor . . . . Rob Hill
Property Storeman. . . . . Marlon Cole
Action Prop Buyer. . . . . Becky Thomas
Chargehand Standby Propman. . . . Brad Torbett
Standby Propman . . . . . Tristan Carlisle-Kitz
Chargehand Dressing Propman . . Laurence Wells
Dressing Propmen. . . . . Mark Geeson
    Gary Robinson   Gregor Telfer
    Richard Magennis   Scott Keery
    Dean Marsh
Practical Electrician . . . . . . Kevin Fitzpatrick
HOD Prop Modeler . . . . . . Duncan McDevitt
Sculptors. . . . . Steve McClure
    Alix Harwood

Prop Modelers . . . . Colin Childs
    Glenn Haddock   Jason Meade
                 Chrissie Overs
Mould Maker . . . . Kevin Walker
Chargehand Prop Painter . . . . . Martin George
Property Trainees . . . . Krysia Whitty
                 Pierre Mendivil
Art Director – Miniatures . . . . . Alastair Bullock
Assistant Art Directors . . . . Peter Dorme
                 David Doran
Draughtsmen . . . . Andrew Palmer
                 Will Coubrough
. . . . Rhys Ifan
Graphic Designers . . . . Laura Dishington
                 Liz Colbert
Junior Draughtsmen . . . . . Catherine Whiting
                 Jo Finkel
Art Department Coordinator . Dominic J Sikking
Graphics Researcher . . . . Olivia Aubry
Art Department Assistants . . . . Kate Pickthall
                 Sarah Ginn
Automaton Manufacturer
. . . . Dick George Creatives Ltd.
Automaton and Horological Advisor . . Michael Start
Train Consultant . . . . Clive Lamming
Camera and Projection Advisor . . Stephen Herbert
Production Buyer . . . . Judy Ducker
Assistant Set Decorators . . . . Zoe Smith
                 Alice Felton
Set Decoration Draughtsman . . . . Remo Tozzi
Assistant Production Buyer . . . . . Kelly Neary
Set Decoration PA . . . . Clare Gosnold
Drapesman . . . . Colin Fox
Costume Supervisor . . . . . . David Davenport
Crowd Supervisor . . . . Marco Scotti
Assistant Costume Designers . . . . Deborah Scott
                 Charlotte Law
. . . . Tim Aslam
Chief Pattern Cutter . . . . . . Melanie Carter
Costume Buyer . . . . Kay Manasseh
Costume Coordinator . . . . . . Caroline Fallon
Principal Costumers . . . . Marco De Magalhaes
                 Sheara Abrahams
Principal Seamstresses . . . . . . Lorraine Burn
                 Trethanna Trevarthen
Chief Crowd Seamstress . . . . Ekaterina Kreinin
Costume Leatherworker . . . Henry Christopher
Costumers . . . . Janine Cunliffe
    Lucille Acevedo Jones   Fola Solanke
    Linda O'Reilly   Lucilla Simbari
                 Oliver Garcia
Principal Costume Trainee . . . . . Kitty Bennett
Costume Trainees . . . . Joel Christopher
                 Maria Cecilia Cafiero

Makeup Designer . . . . Morag Ross
Makeup & Hair Designer to Sir Ben Kingsley
. . . . Anni Buchanan
Key Makeup Artist . . . . Kate Benton
Makeup PA . . . . Emilie Yong
Makeup Crowd Supervisor . . . . . Nicola Buck
Makeup Artists . . . . Polly Fehily
                 Mandy Gold
Makeup Trainees . . . . Angela Kiely
                 Robb Crafer
Hair Designer . . . . Jan Archibald
Key Hairdresser . . . . Bee Archer
Hair Crowd Supervisor . . . . . Barbara Taylor
Hairdresser to Sir Ben Kingsley . Suzanne Stokes-
                 Munton
Crowd Hair PA . . . . Pascale Recher
Hairdressers . . . . Gary Machin
    Rachael Speke   Ann Townsend
                 Rose Warder
Barber . . . . Eric Scruby
Researcher/Consultant . . . . . Marianne Bower
Script Supervisor . . . . Martha Pinson
Dialect Coach . . . . Tim Monich
Stills Photographer . . . . Jaap Buitendijk
Unit Publicist . . . . Larry Kaplan
Assistant Production Coordinator
. . . . Bertie Spiegelberg
Travel & Accommodation Coordinator
. . . . Karl Caffrey
Production Secretary . . . . . . Declan O'Brien
Animal Trainers . . . . Mathilde de Cagny
                 Agni Horak
Assistants to Mr. Scorsese . . . . . Lisa Frechette
                 Tommaso Colognese
Assistants to Mr. King . . . . . Leah Williams
                 Michelle Reed
Assistant to Mr. Headington . . . . Darryl Davy
Assistants to Mr. Crockett . . . . . Rob Brown
                 Tamazin Simmonds
Assistant to Ms. Tillinger Koskoff
. . . . Sheerin Khosrowshahi-miandoab
Assistant to Ms. Kacandes . . . . . Nathan Kelly
Assistant to Sir Ben Kingsley . . . Todd Hofacker
Assistant to Mr. Baron Cohen . . Rhonda George
Key Production Office Assistant . David Coupland
Production Office Assistants . . . . Anna Wilton
                 Rachel Thompson-Nartey
Co-2nd Assistant Directors . . . . Tom Brewster
                 Fraser Fennell-Ball
Crowd Second Assistant Director Candy Marlowe
Third Assistant Directors . . . . . Tania Gordon
    Sandrine Loisy   Danielle Bennett
Set Production Assistants . . . . . Josh Muzaffer
                 Barnaby Riggs

Lock-Off PA's . . . . Tristan Battersby
    Matt Storey   Eleanor Hall
    Teariki Leonard   Hannah Roose
Production Accountant . . . . . Claire Robertson
Payroll Accountants . . . . Karen Bicknell
                       Kathy Ewings
Assistant Accountants . . . . Neil Pierson
    Donna Casey   Will O'Toole
                       Lucy Howell
Hugo Cabret Double . . . . Gary Gannon
Isabelle Double . . . . Honor Saunders
Hugo Cabret Stand-in . . . . . . Maddy Couch
Isabelle Stand-in . . . . Kate Phillips
Construction Manager . . . . Brian Neighbour
Assistant Construction Manager . . . Dave Pearce
Construction Coordinator . . . . . Nancy Scott
Construction Buyer . . . . Mark Russell
HOD Carpenter . . . . Dennis Bovington
Supervising Carpenter . . . . Rob Park
Chargehand Carpenters . . . . . Charlie Gaynor
                   David Perschky
Chargehand Wood Machinist . . . . Karl George
HOD Painter . . . . Gary Crosby
Supervising Painter . . . . Dean Dunham
Chargehand Painters . . . . Craig Gleeson
    Ronald Lattimore   Ben Crosby
HOD Plasterer . . . . Kenny Barley
Supervising Plasterer . . . . . . Micky Gardiner
Chargehand Plasterers . . Christopher Greenwood
                    Steve Court
HOD Sculptor . . . . Emma Jackson
HOD Rigger . . . . Keith Perry
Supervising Rigger . . . . Danny Madden
Chargehand Rigger . . . . Simon Cullen
Riggers . . . . Colin Smith
                       Jon Harris
Trainee Rigger . . . . Sam Sargent
HOD Stagehand . . . . Steve Malin
Chargehand Stagehand . . . . . . Terry Newvell
Stagehands . . . . John Chamberlain
    Keith Muir   Clive Drinkall
Stagehand Labourers . . . . . Darren Connock
                    Joe Bovington

SECOND UNIT

2nd Unit Director / Director of Photography
. . . . Rob Legato
First Assistant Director . . . . Toby Hosking
Third Assistant Director . . . . . Emily Perowne
Art Director . . . . Ashley Winter
First Assistant Camera . . . . Bebe Dierken
I.O. / Convergence Puller . . . . . . John Evans
3D Camera Systems Engineer . . . . . Ross Fall
Script Supervisor . . . . Diana Dill
Key Grip . . . . Keith Mead

Gaffer . . . . Avelino Fernandez
Set Costumer . . . . Helen Ingham
Hairdresser . . . . Morag Smith
Makeup . . . . Kerin Parfitt
Standby Propman . . . . Mat Bergel
Production Sound Mixer . . . . . Martin Seeley
Lead Senior Special Effects Technician
. . . . Steve Paton
Video Assist Operator . . . . Lizzie Kelly

PARIS UNIT

Line Producer . . . . John Bernard
Production Manager – Paris . . . . Michael Sharp
First Assistant Director . . . . Ali Cherkaoui
Production Manager . . . . Gilles Castera
Art Director . . . . Stéphane Cressend
Extras Casting . . . . Aurélie Avram
Crowd Costume Supervisor
. . . . François-Louis Delfolie
Key Makeup . . . . Florence Cossutta
Makeup Crowd Supervisor . . . . Deborah Jarvis
Key Hair . . . . Bettina Miquaix
Chief Lighting Technician . . . . Michaël Monod
Key Grip . . . . Antonin Gendre
Location Manager . . . . Jérôme Boussier
Production Coordinator . . Agnès Berméjo Lainé
Production Accountant . . Emmanuelle Balestrieri
Set Decorator Buyer . . . . . . Emmanuel Délis
Construction Manager . . . . . Ludovic Erbelding
Picture Vehicles Coordinator . . . Charles Heidet
Transportation Coordinator . . . . Jérôme Servant
Music Composed, Orchestrated & Conducted by
. . . . Howard Shore
Music Recorded and Mixed by
. . . . . Simon Rhodes at Abbey Road Studios
Supervising Score Editor . . . . . Jonathan Schultz
Music Technology and Programming
. . . . James Sizemore
Score Editors . . . . Kirsty Whalley
    Rob Houston   Yann McCullough
Production Manager
. . . . . Elizabeth Cotnoir, Eventone Editorial
Production Coordinator . . . . Alan Frey
Music Coordinator . . . . Karen Elliott
Conforming and Auricle . . . . . Tim Starnes
Music Preparation . . . . Amy Baer
    Vic Fraser   Joshua Green
                Jeremy Howard Beck
Orchestra Contracting . . . . . . Isobel Griffiths
Production Accounting . . . . . . Rich Palecek
Post Production Supervisor . . . . Kelley Cribben
Colourist . . . . Greg Fisher
Assistant Editor . . . . Red Charyszyn
Dialogue Editors . . . . Philip Stockton
                Branka Mrkic-Tana

Sound Designer/FX Editor . . . . Eugene Gearty
Supervising ADR Editor . . . . Marissa Littlefield
Foley Supervisor. . . . . Frank Kern
Foley Editors. . . . . Kam Chan
Jamie Baker
Foley Artist. . . . . Marko Costanzo
Foley Recording Engineer . . . . . . George Lara
2nd Assistant Sound Engineer . . Gisburg Smialek
First Assistant Sound Editor . . . . . Chris Fielder
FX Assistant . . . . Sam Miille
Assistant Music Editor. . . . . Ben Pedersen
ADR Assistant Editor. . . . . Angela Organ
Apprentice Sound Editor . . . . Clemence Stoloff
Sound Intern . . . . Silvano Pinto
Post Production Assistants . . . . . Nick Ramirez
Craig Charland
Re-Recorded at . . . . Soundtrack F/T
Recordist . . . . Bret Johnson
Post Production Sound Facility
. . . . C5 Inc., New York
ADR Recorded at . . Sound One Corp., New York
. . . . Goldcrest Post, London
Loop Group Casting
. . . . Brendan Donnison, Lyps Inc.
Dailies Stereo Correction Artist . . . Victor Riva
Dailies Digital 3D Lab Manager . . . Janine Abery
Digital Intermediate and Digital Cinema provided by
. . . . Technicolor
Digital Intermediate Producer . . Marisa Clayton
Digital Intermediate Conform & Color Support
. . . . Katie Largay
Digital Intermediate Engineering & Color Science
Thomas Overton   Joe Beirne
Doug Jaqua   Bill "BT" Topazio
Technical Support NY
. . . . Technicolor – Postworks NY
Stereo Digital Intermediate
. . . . CAMERON | PACE Group
Post Stereo Supervisor . . . . Dave Watro
Stereo Workflow Supervisor . . Derek Schweickart
Stereo Correction Specialists
Mark Todd Osborne   Rick Ives
Titles Designed and Produced by
. . . . Big Film Design
Title Designer . . . . Randall Ballsmeyer
Titles Compositor . . . . Eddie Porter
Titles Stereographer. . . . . . . Jonathan Skabla
Digital Image Restoration
. . . . Technicolor Restoration Services
Restoration Director . . . . Tom Burton
Lead Restoration Artist . . . . . . Danny Albano
Restoration Team. . . . . Joe Zarceno
Trey Freeman   John Healy
Mike Underwood

Archival Footage Stereo Conversion Services
provided by Legend 3D
Archival Conversion Supervisor . . Jared Sandrew
Archival Conversion Producer . . . . . Matt Akey
Archival Conversion Stereographer . . . Jill Hunt
Production Supervisor . . . . Tyler Bennink
Lead Depth Artist . . . . Kim Mandilag
Visual Effects Supervisor . . . . . Ben Grossmann
Visual Effects Producer . Karen Murphy-Mundell
Digital Effects Supervisor. . . . . . Alex Henning
Visual Effects Data Supervisor . . . Giles Harding
Visual Effect Editors . . . . . Javier Marcheselli
Kosta Saric
Encoder Technicians . . . . Tomi Keeling
Ian Menzies
Visual Effects Video Assist . . . . . Adrian Spanna
Visual Effects Coordinators . . . . Katrina Barton
Brenda Finster
Visual Effects Assistants . . . . . Anthony Bowden
Katherine Legato
Visual Effects by. . . . . Pixomondo
Executive Producer . . . . Thilo Kuther
CG Supervisor . . . . Adam Watkins
Visual Effects Producer . . . . . Jonathan Stone
Digital Producer . . . . Natasha Ozoux
Senior Visual Effects Coordinator . . . Perry Kain
Art Direction . . . . . . Ingo Putze, Rick Rische
Head of Pipeline . . . . Patrick Wolf
Division Supervisors. . . . . Fabio Zangla
Sven Martin   Saku Partamies
Mihaela Orzea   Simon Britnell
Chris Stenner   Damian Doennig
Pieter Mientz   Jörn Großhans
Benjamin Seide   Robert Zeltsch
Colin Brady   Juri Stanossek
Kenny Tam
Division Producers . . . . . . Steven McKendry
Lisa Hansen   Jing Li
Franzisca Puppe   Jan Fielder
Christoph Zollinger   Paul King
Armando Plata
Lead Artists / Technical Directors
Dider Muanza   Martin Wellstein
Mahmoud Rahnama   Xiaowei Weng
Luca Zappala   Oliver Zangenberg
Steven Hansen   Miodrag Colombo
Roger Gibbon   Rodrigo Teixeria
Martin Jurado   Runlin Xiong
Klaus Wuchta   Lance Ranzer
Miguel Diaz Cachero   Leo Jia
Jan Adamczyk   Tzuen Wu
Enrico Damm   Sebastian Butenberg
Division Editors   Brian Miller
Duncan Rochfort   Tobias Pfeiffer

CG Artists . . . . Chris Chang
Iacopo Di Luigi   Leszek Plichta
Stefan Willisch   Dean Faulder
Irina Bennoit   Lon Krung
Sven Muller   Emanuele Paris
Jin-Ho Jeon   Marc Hankel
Tobias Dommer   Greg Szafranski
John Schratz   Marc Joos
Tobias Gruenberger   Eric Kasanowski
Justin Zhu   Norman Krüsmann
Xiaogang Qi   Hamza Butt
Kai Lin   Rens Heeren
Yingchun Cao   Heng Liu
Katie Talbot   Sally Wilson
Zhuotao Zhang
Lighting / Shading / Texturing
. . . . Alessandro Sabbioni
Irfan Celik   Jürgen Bilstein
Sean Raffel   Alexander Hupperich
Jiabin Tan   Lesley Rooney
Simon Lower Greg Meeres-Young Jonas
Noell   Markus Graf
Tilo Spalke   Tyler Esselstrom
Animators . . . . Ana Maria Alvarado
Florian Friedmann   Stephen Baker
                       Ingo Schachner
Compositors . . . . Abigail Scollay
Franz Brandstätter   Linus Burghardt
Qian Han   Ando Avila
Gunnar Heiss   Liwen Liu
Richard Frazer   Anthony Kramer
Gwen Zhang   Marion Voignier
Rickey Verma   Benjamin Scabell
Ivan Kokov   Mark Joey Tang
Ricky Cheung   Caroline Pires
Jan Oberhauser   Mark Pinheiro
Sebastian Bommersheim Chen Sun
Jason Bidwell   Martin Tallosy
Sören Volz   Christian Stadach
Jianghong Zhu   Max Riess
Stephan Schaefholz   Christoph Metzger
Jiarun Zou   Micah Gallagher
Stephanie Saillard   Darren Christie
Johannes Bogenhauser   Michael Vorberg
Tobias Wiesner   Denny Ertanto
John Brubaker   Moritz Strothmann
Tommaso Fioretti   Ebru Gönül
John Dinh   Nina Pries
Torsten Neuendorf   Ed Plant
Jonas Stuckenbrock   Noemie Cruciani
Toshiko Miura   Emma Brofjorden
Karen Cheng   Noll Linsangan
Travis Nobles   Elena Topouzoglou
Kataryzna Ancuta   Patrick Kreuser

Wenkang Li   Eva Kniel
Larkin Flynn   Philip Lücke
Xinguo Zou   Florian Franke
Le Zhang   Philip Nussbaumer
Xuzhen An   Zhixin Zhang
FX Artists . . . . Maria Eugenia Ocantos
Marcel Kern   Tobias Ott
Michal Maciejewski   Boris Bruchhaus
                       Leon Loukeris
Character / Rigging / Massive . . . Justin Lewers
Oscar Medina   Walter Schultz
                       Katja Federkiel
Matte Painting / Environment Artists . . . .
Adam Figielski   David Fonseca
Martin Höhnle   Rene Borst
Adam Wesierski   Istvan Veress Kovacs
Max Dennison   Robert Kriegel
Alex Nice   Jerome Fournier
Metin Gungor   Roger Kupelian
Darren Quah   Marco Wilz
Paul Campion   Sven Sauer
Mariusz Wesierski   Rainer Stolle
Thilo Ewers   Bjørn Mayer
Division Coordinators . . . . Viktorija Ogureckaja
Phi Van Le   Oliver Arnold
Bill Wang   Yvette Shum
Frederick Cholewa   Shanshan Xie
Yonrong Yu   Alessandra Serrano
Katharina Keßler   Momo Zhan
Marlies Schacherl
Matchmove / Layout Artists . . . Azzard Gordon
Gareth Stevenson   Lukas Niklaus
Xiaoyong Hu   Ben Sharp
Hsuanyi Fang   Maeve Eydmann
Yong Cheng   Chao He
Jialin Su   Peng Zhang
Zhennan Quan   Chenchen Ma
Johannes Weiss   Thierry Hamel
Zhongwei Chen   Emerick Tackett
Joseph Eapen   Tricia Kim
Zihao Zhang   Feiyi Wei
Konstantinos Pontikidis Vanja Jozinovic
Li Li   Wei Zhang
Roto / Paint Artists . . . . Annalyn Betinol
Dongyue Yang   Jeanette Monero
Stephen Edwards   Benson Guo
Doris Ding   Kaifeng Wei
Wally Chin   Cheng Cheng
Hongyan Ji   Laura Jacobs
Yanlin Wang   Cristina Vozian
Huajing Zhuo   Salahuddin Razul
Zhao Yang   Crystal Schrecengost
Jaroslaw Ancuta   Simia Song
                       Zofie Olsson

Production Assistants . . . . . . Genevieve Claire
    Jesse Looney   Irene Martin
                      Siyun Yi
Visual Effects by. . . . . Lola VFX
    Edson Williams   Holly Alvarado
    Trent Claus   Erik Bruhwiler
    Scott Balkcom   Max Leonard
    Jeremiah Sweeney   Brian Hajek
    Thomas Nittman   Rob Olsson
    Casey Allen   Josh Singer
Visual Effects and Digital Environments
created by . . . . Uncharted Territory
    Volker Engel   Marc Weigert
    Rony Soussan   Joseph M. Harkins
    Ryan Smolarek   Pieter Van Houte
    Talon Nightshade   Patrick Mullane
    Hannes Poser   Conrad Murrey
    Ron Griswold   Jack Ghoulian
    Tony Meagher   Katharina Koepke
    Julia Smola   Kohl Harrington
    Dennis Murillo   John Vaughan
Opening Shot by
Industrial Light and Magic, A Lucasfilm Ltd. Company
Visual Effects Supervisor. . . . . . . John Knoll
Matte Painting Supervision and
Visual Effects by . . . . . . Matte World Digital
    Craig Barron   Ken Rogerson
    Todd R. Smith   Erin Collins Butler
    Morgan Trotter   Cameron Noble
    Donna Sousa   Brian Berringer
    Geeta Basantani   Chris Evans
                 Leonid Kogan
     Daphne Apellanes-Ackerson
    Eric Hamel   John Goodson
                 Britton Taylor
     Annemieke Loomis Hutchins
    Julien Dupuy   Derek Kraus
    Chris Stoski   Thomas Maksymowiz
              Shuichi Yoshida
Previsualization by . . NVIZAGE Previsualization
Previs Supervisor . . . . Martin Chamney
Lead Previs Artist. . . . . Michelle Blok
Previs Artists . . . . Matt Gibson
                 Mike Gilbert
Virtual Camera Developer . . . Hugh Macdonald
Virtual Camera Operator. . . . . Stuart Haskayne
Miniatures and Additional Visual Effects
Photography
New Deal Studios
Supervisor . . . . Matthew Gratzner
Producer. . . . . David Sanger
Location Manager . . . . Jamie Lengyel
Location Assistants . . . . Paul Tomlinson
                 Barney Pearce

Unit Manager. . . . . Simon Crook
UK Casting. . . . . Susie Parriss
                 Rose Wicksteed
Casting Associate . . . . Meghan Rafferty
Australia Casting. . . . . Christine King
Extras Casting . . . Tara Keenan @ 2020 Casting
Caterer . . . . Chorley Bunce
Magic Consultant and Instructor. . . . Paul Kieve
Choreographer . . . . Diana Scrivener
Tutor to Mr. Butterfield. . . . . Charles Howes
Tutor to Miss Moretz. . . Laura "Sissie" Torrance
Cast Tutor . . . . Katherine Hook
Unit Nurse . . . . Jeanie Udall
Health & Safety . . . . Mick Hurrell
                 Malcolm Pearce
Stage Security . . . . . Ian Pearce, Len Steadman
Fire Officer . . . . Derek Warman
Post Production Accountant . . . . . Liz Modena
                 Trevanna Post Inc.
Production Insurance provided by
  . . . Gallagher Entertainment Insurance Services
    Arthur J. Gallagher & Co. Insurance Brokers of
                 California, Inc.
Music Legal and Clearance by
  . . . . . . Christine Bergren Music Consulting
  . . . . . . Christine Bergren, Allison Cumming
Rights and Clearances by
  . . . . Entertainment Clearances, Inc.
        Cassandra Barbour, Laura Sevier
Legal Services provided by . . . . . Olswang LLP
                 Kaye Scholer LLP
Production Services France . . . . Peninsula Film
Additional Production Financing provided by
. . . . Union Bank, N.A.
Dolby Sound Consultant. . . . . Steve F.B. Smith
Lighting Services supplied by . . . . Panalux
Filmed at
SHEPPERTON & PINEWOOD STUDIOS,
London at LONGCROSS STUDIOS, Surrey,
England and on location in PARIS, France
Soundtrack Album on Howe Records

MUSIC

ÇA GAZE
Composed by V. Marceau
Produced by Jean Michel Bernard
Performed by Les Primitifs du Futur

FROU FROU
Words by Marie Blondeau, Henri Custillon and
Hector Monreal
Music by Henri Chatau and Lucien Dormel
Performed by Lucille Panis
Courtesy of Sony Music Entertainment
By arrangement with Sony Music Licensing

CARINOSA
Written by Alberto Larena and Auguste Pesenti
Conducted by Howard Shore

AUBADE CHARMEUSE
Written by Jean Peyronnin
Produced by Jean Michel Bernard
Performed by Les Primitifs du Futur

CARINOSA
Written by Alberto Larena and Auguste Pesenti
Produced by Jean Michel Bernard
Performed by Les Primitifs du Futur
Score excerpts from the motion picture *SAFETY LAST*
Composed by Carl Davis
Courtesy of Fremantle Media

TARANTELLA
Written by Camille Saint-Saëns
Arranged by Howard Shore

DANSE MACABRE
Written by Camille Saint-Saëns
Arranged by Howard Shore

FRIENDLY DAY
Written and Performed by Kevin MacLeod

SI TU VEUX MARGUERITE
Written by Albert Valensi and Joseph Vincentelli
Produced by Jean Michel Bernard
Performed by Olivier Constantin and
Jean Michel Bernard

MARCHE DE RADETZKY
Composed by Johann Strauss Sr.
Produced by Doug Adams
Courtesy of Jasper and Marian Sanfilippo and the
Sanfilippo Foundation.
Recorded from a 1908 Limonaire Orchestrophone
- Style 250, built in Paris, France

BY THE WATERS OF THE MINNETONKA
Written by James M. Cavanass and
Thurlow Lieurance
Performed by Zez Confrey
Courtesy of Warner Classics
By arrangement with Warner Music Group Film
& TV Licensing

SIX GNOSSIENNES: NO. 1 LENT
Written by Erik Satie
Performed by Aldo Ciccolini
Courtesy of EMI Music France
Under license from EMI Film & Television Music

DARDANELLA
Written by Felix Bernard, Johnny S. Black and Fred Fisher
Performed by Paul Eakins Mortier Belgian Band Organ
Courtesy of Carlisle Music Company

TROIS MORCEAUX EN FORME DE POIRE:
MANIÈRE DE COMMENCEMENT (*ALLEZ MODÉRÉMENT*)
Written by Erik Satie
Performed by Aldo Ciccolini & Gabriel Tacchino
Courtesy of EMI Music France
Under license from EMI Film & Television Music

COEUR VOLANT
Word and Music by Elizabeth Cotnoir, Isabelle
Geffroy and Howard Shore
Performed by Zaz
Courtesy of Play On
Les Primitifs du Futur:
Dominque Cravic, Hervé Legeay, Romane, Jean-
Phillippe Viret, Mathilde Febrer, Daniel Colin

**Footage from films by
GEORGES MÉLIÈS**
VOYAGE DANS LA LUNE (*Trip to the Moon*)
LE ROI DU MAQUILLAGE (*Untamable Whiskers*)
À LA CONQUÊTE DU PÔLE (*The Conquest of the Pole*)
LE MÉLOMANE (*The Melomaniac*)
LE ROYAUME DES FÉES (*Kingdom of Fairies*)
PAPILLON FANTASTIQUE (*Spider and the Butterfly*)
LA FÉE CARABOSSE OU LE POIGNARD FATAL (*The Witch*)
LES ILLUSIONS FANTAISISTES (*Whimsical Illusions*)
VOYAGE À TRAVERS L'IMPOSSIBLE (*Impossible Journey*)
Courtesy of Lobster Films
LES QUAT' CENTS FARCES DU DIABLE (*The Merry Frolics of Satan*)
Courtesy of EYE Film Institute Netherlands
THE TRIP TO THE MOON
Original Color Version
Film by Georges Méliès (1902)
Restored by Lobster Films,
Groupama Gan Foundation for Cinema and
Technicolor
Foundation for Cinema Heritage
with participation of Madeleine Malthête - Méliès
and the Centre National de la Cinématographie –
CNC
THE TRIP TO THE MOON
Restored Color Version ©2011 Lobster Films /
Groupama Gan Foundation for Cinema /
Technicolor Foundation for Cinema Heritage
Recreated sets, props and drawings from

films and works by
GEORGES MÉLIÈS
LE PALAIS DES MILLE ET UNE NUITS(The
Palace of a Thousand and One Nights)
FAUST AUX ENFERS (The Damnation of Faust)
ÉCLIPSE DE SOLEIL EN PLEINE LUNE (The
Eclipse: Courtship of the Sun and Moon)
LES QUAT' CENTS FARCES DU DIABLE
(The Merry Frolics of Satan)
LE CAKE-WALK INFERNAL (The Infernal
Cakewalk)
LE RAID PARIS – MONTE-CARLO EN
DEUX HEURES (Paris to Monte Carlo)
CENDRILLON (Cinderella)
LA LIBELLULE (The Dragon Fly)
LE CAUCHEMAR (A Nightmare)
L'HOMME À LA TÊTE EN CAOUTCHOUC (
The Man with the Exploding Head)
LA CHRYSALIDE ET LE PAPILLON D'OR
(The Brahmin and the Butterfly)
LE MENUET LILLIPUTIEN (The Lilliputian
Minuet)
GROTTE AVEC FLAMMES (Cave with Flames)
LA DIFTHIGIJIKA (Among the Circassians)

Silent Films
World War I Footage
Courtesy of Gaumont Pathe' Archives
London Street footage 1903
Courtesy of BFI National Archive
Lumière Clips
SORTIE D'USINE, 1895
ARRIVÉE D'UN TRAIN À LA CIOTAT, 1897
Coll. Institut Lumière - © Association frères
Lumière
SAFETY LAST
Courtesy of Harold Lloyd Entertainment, Inc.
DAS CABINET DES DR. CALIGARI
(Cabinet of Dr. Caligari) Robert Wiene
Rights: Friedrich-Wilhelm-Murnau-Stiftung
Distributor: Transit Film GmbH
THE FOUR HORSEMAN OF THE
APOCALYPSE
Licensed by Warner Bros Entertainment Inc. and
Turner Entertainment Co.
LA FILLE DE L'EAU (Whirlpool of Fate)
© 1924 Studiocanal Courtesy of Studiocanal
THE KID by Charles Chaplin
Motion Picture:
Copyright © 1921 Roy Export S.A.S.
All Rights Reserved.
Renewed:
Copyright © 1948 Roy Export S.A.S.
All Rights Reserved.

DIE BÜCHSE DER PANDORA (Pandora's Box)
Courtesy of Janus Films
THE GENERAL
THE THIEF OF BAGDAD
TUMBLEWEEDS
Courtesy of Film Preservation Associates, Inc.
THE GREAT TRAIN ROBBERY
INTOLERANCE
HELL'S HINGES
Courtesy of The Museum of Modern Art, New
York
DICKSON EXPERIMENTAL SOUND FILM
CORBETT AND COURTNEY BEFORE THE
KINETOGRAPH
MAY IRWIN KISS
Courtesy of Library of Congress
Posters Courtesy of
Serodent,
Eau de Cologne No. 555 by Leonetto Cappiello
Au Bon Marche by Jean Carlu
Cora Madou, Tabarin by Paul Colin
À la conquête du pôle by Jacques Faria
L'Operateur, Le Million,
and *À Nous La Liberte* by Jean-Adrien Mercier
© Artists Rights Society (ARS),
New York / ADAGP, Paris
Gitanes Cigarettes by Marcello Dudovich,
© Artists Rights Society (ARS),
New York / SIAE, Rome
by Victor Jean Desmeures
Musee de l'Armee/
© National Museum of
History and Culture of Immigration, CNHI
Lumiere Cinematographe London 1896
Le Cinematographe – Grand Café, 28 Dec 1895
Coll. Institut Lumière - © Association frères
Lumière

Fantomas
Courtesy of Gaumont S.A.
A.M. Cassandre artwork © Mouron.
Cassandre Lic 2010-14-06-02
www.cassandre-france.com
NESTLÉ is a registered trademark
of Societe' des Produits Nestle' S. A.
Vevey, Switzerland

Additional archival and film materials provided by
Dominique Besson
Jean-Louis Capitaine
Estate of Charles Chaplin, Bubbles Incorporated
S.A.
Corbis Corporation: Pierre
Vauthey/Sygma/National Geographic Society/

Hulton-Deutsch Collection
Getty Images: Popperfoto/Roger-Violett/Hulton
Archive/Archive Photos/ Redferns
Roger-Violett/Maurice Branger
Imperial War Museum / Gilbert Rogers IWM
3819
World Media Rights, London
Thanks
Athénée Théâtre Louis Jouvet
Bibliothèque Sainte-Geneviève
BFI
Cinematheque Francaise
Groupama - Square de l'Opéra Louis Jouvet, Paris
La Sorbonne
Victoria & Albert Museum, London

Additional Acknowledgments

Jehanne d'Alcy	Jean Renoir
Catherine Hessling	Jean Eugène Robert-Houdin
Raoul Arter	Marquise De Sévigné
	August Leymarie
Adrien Barrere	Alexandre Falguière
	Alphonse Mucha
Herbert Bayer	Florit
	Manuel Orazi
Bernard Becan	Louis Gaudin
	Raymond Pallier
Paul Berthon	Charles Gesmar
	Paul Philippoteaux
Djo Bourgeois	Ferdinand Hart-Nibbrig
	Plumereau
Cechheto Paul Iribe	Armand Rapeno
Jean Chaboseau	Robert Kastor
	Henri Roberty
Jules Cheret	Maurice Lauro
	Georgii et Vladimir Stenberg
Candido Aragonese de Faria	Lingi
	Francisco Tamagno
David Dellepiane	Lion Noir
	Vaillant
Henri Desfontaines	Stephané Lallemant
	René Vincent
Daniel De Losques	Georges Leonnec
	Kurt Wenzel

Special Thanks
Madeleine Malthête-Méliès
Marie-Hélène Leherissey-Méliès
Jacques Malthête
Pauline Duclaud-Lacoste
Helen Morris Scorsese

Ariel Emanuel
Rick Yorn
Christopher Donnelly
Laurent Mannoni
Mark McElhatten
Gina Telaroli
Russell Borrill

Makeup Provided by M.A.C. Cosmetics
GRS Systems, Inc.
Gregg Paliotta and Michael Johnston, Digital
Media Systems Inc.
GK FILMS DID NOT RECEIVE ANY PAY-
MENT OR OTHER CONSIDERATION,
OR ENTER INTO ANY AGREEMENT, FOR
THE DEPICTION OF TOBACCO PROD-
UCTS IN THIS FILM.
Color and Prints by DELUXE ®
Captured with ALEXA
(Logo)   (Logo)
Fusion 3D technology provided by CAMERON |
PACE Group   Union Bank (Logo)
(Logo)
MPAA Globe # 47203
DOLBY SDDS   DATASAT
(Logo) (Digital)   (Logo)
(Logo)

Copyright © 2011 GK Films, LLC.
All Rights Reserved.
All material is protected by Copyright Laws of the
United States and all countries throughout the
world.
Country of First Publication: United States of
America.
GK Films, LLC is the author of this motion pic-
ture for the purposes of copyright and other laws.
Any unauthorized exhibition, distribution or
copying of this film or any part thereof (including
soundtrack) is an infringement of the relevant
copyright and will subject the infringer to severe
civil and criminal penalties.
The story, all names, characters and incidents por-
trayed in this production are fictitious.
No identification with actual persons, places,
buildings and products is intended or should be
inferred.
GK FILMS
Static logo
PARAMOUNT PICTURES
Static logo

About the Filmmakers

MARTIN SCORSESE (Directed by / Produced by) was born in 1942 in New York City, and was raised in the neighborhood of Little Italy, which later provided the inspiration for several of his films. Scorsese earned a B.S. degree in film communications in 1964, followed by an M.A. in the same field in 1966 at New York University's School of Film. During this time, he made numerous prize-winning short films including *The Big Shave*. In 1968, Scorsese directed his first feature film, entitled *Who's That Knocking At My Door?*

He served as assistant director and an editor of the documentary *Woodstock* in 1970 and won critical and popular acclaim for his 1973 film *Mean Streets*. Scorsese directed his first documentary film, *Italianamerican,* in 1974. In 1976, Scorsese's *Taxi Driver* was awarded the Palme d'Or at the Cannes Film Festival. He followed with *New York, New York* in 1977, *The Last Waltz* in 1978 and *Raging Bull* in 1980, which received eight Academy Award® nominations, including Best Picture and Best Director. Scorsese went on to direct *The Color of Money, The Last Temptation of Christ, Goodfellas, Cape Fear, Casino, Kundun,* and *The Age of Innocence,* among other films.

In 1996, Scorsese completed a four-hour documentary, *A Personal Journey With Martin Scorsese Through American Movies,* co-directed by Michael Henry Wilson. The documentary was commissioned by the British Film Institute to celebrate the 100th anniversary of the birth of cinema.

In 2001 Scorsese released *Il Mio Viaggio in Italia,* an epic documentary that affectionately chronicles his love for Italian Cinema. His long-cherished project, *Gangs of New York,* was released in 2002, earning numerous critical honors, including a Golden Globe Award for Best Director. In 2003, PBS broadcast the seven-film documentary series *Martin Scorsese Presents: The Blues. The Aviator* was released in December of 2004 and earned five Academy Awards®, in addition to the Golden Globe and BAFTA awards for Best Picture. In 2005, *No Direction Home: Bob Dylan* was broadcast as part of the *American Masters* series on PBS. In 2006, *The Departed* was released to critical acclaim and was honored with the Director's Guild of America, Golden Globe, New York Film Critics, National Board of Review and Critic's Choice awards for Best Director, in addition to four Academy Awards®, including Best Picture and Best Director. Scorsese's documentary of the Rolling Stones in concert, *Shine a Light,* was released in 2008. In February 2010, *Shutter Island* premiered. That year, Scorsese also released two documentaries: the Peabody Award-winning *A Letter to Elia* on PBS; and *Public Speaking,* starring writer Fran Lebowitz on HBO. In October 2011, Scorsese's documentary for HBO, *George Harrison: Living in the Material World,* was released.

Scorsese also serves as executive producer on HBO's series *Boardwalk Empire*, for which he directed the pilot episode. The series went on to win the Golden Globe for Best Television Series Drama and Scorsese took home the DGA Award for Outstanding Directorial Achievement in a Dramatic Series.

Scorsese's additional awards and honors include the Golden Lion from the Venice Film Festival (1995), the AFI Life Achievement Award (1997), the Honoree at the Film Society of Lincoln Center's 25th Gala Tribute (1998), the DGA Lifetime Achievement Award (2003), The Kennedy Center Honors (2007), and the HFPA Cecil B. DeMille Award (2010).

Scorsese is the founder and chair of The Film Foundation, a non-profit organization dedicated to the preservation and protection of motion picture history. At the 2007 Cannes Film Festival, Scorsese launched the World Cinema Foundation, a not-for-profit organization dedicated to the preservation and restoration of neglected films from around the world, with special attention paid to those developing countries lacking the financial and technical resources to do the work themselves. Scorsese is the founder and chair.

JOHN LOGAN (Screenplay by) is an acclaimed Tony Award-winning dramatist and Academy Award®-nominated screenwriter, whose works span a multitude of genres, from dramas and comedies, to action and animated films. Logan is often hailed for his remarkable ability to capture the voice of the character while transporting viewers into accessible worlds rich with color. Logan's films have garnered a worldwide box office total of nearly $2 billion—making him one of the most successful and sought-after screenwriters in the industry.

In January 2012, the Weinstein Company released John Logan's modern-day film adaptation of Shakespeare's *Coriolanus,* a tragedy based on the life of the legendary Roman leader, Gaius Marcius Coriolanus. Ralph Fiennes directs and stars in the film, opposite Gerard Butler, Vanessa Redgrave, and Jessica Chastain.

Logan penned the next James Bond film, *Skyfall,* with Daniel Craig reprising the role of Bond, and also stars Javier Bardem and Ralph Fiennes, with Sam Mendes directing. Sony is set to release the film in the fall of 2012. Logan is also collaborating with Patti Smith on adapting the film version of her best-selling book, *Just Kids*, which chronicles the musician's early years in New York.

In 2000, Logan earned global recognition and his first Academy Award® nomination for Best Original Screenplay for *Gladiator*, which went on to win five Oscars®, including Best Picture. The script, which illustrated Logan's ability to combine visceral action sequences with poetic tenderness, earned Logan both BAFTA and WGA nominations. In 2004, Logan received his second Academy Award® nomination for *The Aviator*, an original screenplay starring Leonardo DiCaprio and directed by Martin Scorsese. The film received a total of 11 nominations and five wins, and resulted in BAFTA, WGA, and Golden Globe nominations for Logan.

Logan's diverse background in film also includes *Rango* (2011), *Sweeney Todd: The Demon Barber of Fleet Street* (2007), *The Last Samurai* (2003), *Sinbad: Legend of the Seven Seas* (2003), *Star Trek: Nemesis* (2002), and *Any Given Sunday* (1999).

In addition to his immensely successful screenwriting career, Logan is an accomplished dramatist with more than a dozen plays to his credit. His play, *Red*, received six Tony Awards in 2010, including the award for Best Play. *Red* premiered at the Donmar Warehouse in London and at the Golden Theatre on Broadway. Logan's other noted plays including *Never the Sinner* and *Hauptmann*, and his adaptation of Ibsen's *The Master Builder*, which premiered in the West End in 2003 to great acclaim.

Acclaimed *New York Times*-bestselling author/illustrator **BRIAN SELZNICK** (Based on the Book Entitled *The Invention of Hugo Cabret* by) graduated from the Rhode Island School of Design with the intention of becoming a set designer for the theater. However, after spending three years selling books and designing window displays for a children's bookstore in Manhattan, he was inspired to create children's books of his own. His books have received many awards and distinctions, including a Caldecott Medal for *The Invention of Hugo Cabret*, a Caldecott Honor for *The Dinosaurs of Waterhouse Hawkins*, and a Robert F. Sibert Honor for *When Marian Sang*. Brian divides his time between Brooklyn, New York, and San Diego, California.

A MARTIN SCORSESE PICTURE

HUGO

PARAMOUNT PICTURES AND GK FILMS PRESENT A GK FILMS/INFINITUM NIHIL PRODUCTION
BEN KINGSLEY   SACHA BARON COHEN   ASA BUTTERFIELD   CHLOË GRACE MORETZ "HUGO" RAY WINSTONE
EMILY MORTIMER WITH JUDE LAW   CASTING BY ELLEN LEWIS   MUSIC SUPERVISOR RANDALL POSTER   MUSIC BY HOWARD SHORE   VISUAL EFFECTS SUPERVISOR ROB LEGATO
COSTUME DESIGNER SANDY POWELL   EDITOR THELMA SCHOONMAKER, A.C.E.   PRODUCTION DESIGNED BY DANTE FERRETTI   DIRECTOR OF PHOTOGRAPHY ROBERT RICHARDSON, ASC
EXECUTIVE PRODUCERS EMMA TILLINGER KOSKOFF   DAVID CROCKETT   GEORGIA KACANDES   CHRISTI DEMBROWSKI   BARBARA DEFINA
PRODUCED BY GRAHAM KING   TIM HEADINGTON   MARTIN SCORSESE   JOHNNY DEPP   BASED ON THE BOOK ENTITLED THE INVENTION OF HUGO CABRET BY BRIAN SELZNICK
SCREENPLAY BY JOHN LOGAN   DIRECTED BY MARTIN SCORSESE   HugoMovie.com

MOTION PICTURE © 2011 GK FILMS, LLC ALL RIGHTS RESERVED.   © 2011 PARAMOUNT PICTURES. ALL RIGHTS RESERVED.

HUGO
THE SHOOTING SCRIPT

Asa Butterfield as Hugo Cabret

"*Hugo,* an utterly beautiful film—both visually and emotionally—and itself an enchanting gift from Scorsese to film fans everywhere....This kind of cinematic delight is a rarity, a warm and masterfully crafted reminder of why we love to go to the movies in the first place."

—Mike Scott, *The Times-Picayune*

"*Hugo* is a fable as sensitive and powerful as any Scorsese film since *The Age of Innocence* nearly two decades ago. Bursting with earned emotion, *Hugo* is a mechanism that comes to life at the turn of a key in the shape of a heart."

—Richard Corliss, *Time*

"In *Hugo,* an exhilarating tale of magic, machines, memories, and dreams, Martin Scorsese pulls off the neatest trick of all. He marshals the marvels of modern movie technology—up to and including the dreaded 3-D—to create a love letter to the earliest of movies and, by extension, to every movie from then to now. ... *Hugo* is based on Brian Selznick's 2007 young-adult novel *The Invention of Hugo Cabret,* an extraordinary work of imagination....Scorsese, screenwriter John Logan, and an army of sympathetic technicians bring the book off the page and into the realm of digitally amplified movie reality."
—Ty Burr, *Boston Globe*

Director Martin Scorsese, the legendary storyteller, invites you to join him on a thrilling journey to a magical world with his first-ever 3D film, from a screenplay by John Logan, based on Brian Selznick's award-winning, imaginative *New York Times* bestseller, *The Invention of Hugo Cabret.*

Hugo is the astonishing adventure of a wily and resourceful boy whose quest to unlock a secret left to him by his father will transform Hugo and all those around him, and reveal a safe and loving place he can call home.

Scorsese has assembled an impressive acting ensemble comprised of rising new talent working alongside venerated stars of the stage and motion pictures, including Ben Kingsley, Sacha Baron Cohen, Asa Butterfield, Chloë Grace Moretz, Ray Winstone, Emily Mortimer, Helen McCrory, Christopher Lee, Richard Griffiths, Frances De La Tour, Michael Stuhlbarg, and with Jude Law.

This Newmarket Shooting Script® Book includes:
- Foreword by Brian Selznick
- Introduction by John Logan
- Script by John Logan, adapted from Brian Selznick's *The Invention of Hugo Cabret*
- Production Notes
- Color photo section—23 stills
- Full cast and crew credits

JOHN LOGAN's work as a screenwriter includes *Hugo, Coriolanus, Rango, Sweeney Todd, The Aviator, Gladiator, The Last Samurai, Any Given Sunday,* and *RKO 281.* He received the Tony, Drama Desk, Outer Critic Circle, and Drama League awards for his play *Red,* and is the author of more than a dozen plays.

newmarket *press* for itbooks
AN IMPRINT OF HARPERCOLLINS PUBLISHERS

Visit our website at **www.newmarketpress.com**.

Movie artwork © 2011 Paramount Pictures Corp.
Pictures copyright © 2011 GK Films LLC.
All rights reserved.

ISBN 978-0-06-220277-2

USA $19.99